CHIAROSCURO AND

Grazia Deledda spent her childh.......ous heart of Sardinia listening to sto.......he servants and guests about the frivolous an.... happy, heart-rending and tragic incidents in the lives of the people; stories that furnished her imagination with material for a lifetime. Her first story, 'Sardinian Blood', was published in Rome when she was sixteen – an auspicious beginning for a prodigious writing career that spanned five decades.

Deledda vowed to make Sardinia better known to the world through her fiction. Rising vividly out of her Sardinian experience, the full-blooded characters are given a stage with realistic backdrops and allowed to tell their story naturally. The characters' self-deceptions and secret (often hopeless) ambitions are revealed through their conversations and inadvertent comments and gestures. The supposedly senile grandfather in 'The Boy in Hiding' outfoxes his more sophisticated and stubborn sons without saying a word. The delinquent schoolboy in 'The Marten' can't keep from stealing the dearest posession of a 'house nun'. Often at the core of these tales is an authentic but irrational fear of the unkown; there are stories of loneliness that lead to disastrous alliances and stories of deceit. 'Chiaroscuro' is an example of how Deledda, without malice or moralizing, depicts the superstitions, fears, beliefs and legends of eighteenth century Sardinia. Caralu dupes his landlady with a string of lies, he makes her suffer but also provides her with something that no one else can, and proves the adage loudly proclaimed by her jilted lover that, given a choice, a woman will always choose a bad man over a good one. Through these stories we enter into the psychology of a wide range of characters belonging to another age, with different ways of coping with and assessing life's inevitable trials. However much their daily lives may differ from ours, we are irrestistibly drawn into their dramas by Deledda's vivid powers of observation and narration.

GRAZIA DELEDDA

Born in 1871 in Nuoro, Sardinia, Grazia Deledda lived
and wrote there until her marriage in 1900, when she
moved to Rome. In 1926, she became the second woman
and second Italian to win the Nobel Prize for Literature.
A great humanitarian and an idealistically inspired
writer, Deledda wrote over thirty novels and many books
of short stories. Most of her work focuses on the world of
the poor, superstitious Sardinian peasantry which was
losing ground to the culture of the middle-class
landlords. She died in 1936.

Her novels *After the Divorce*, *Cosima* and *Elias Portolu*
are also published in the Quartet Encounters series.

GRAZIA DELEDDA

Chiaroscuro and Other Stories

Translated from the Italian and with an Introduction by
MARTHA KING

QUARTET ENCOUNTERS
Quartet Books

First published in Great Britain by Quartet Books
Limited 1994
A member of the Namara Group
27 Goodge Street
London W1P 1FD

Translation copyright © Martha King 1994

ISBN 0 7043 0213 6

A catalogue record for this title is available from the
British Library

Printed and bound in Finland by WSOY

Contents

Introduction

Grazia Deledda (1871–1936), Nobel Prize winner for literature in 1926, began writing and publishing at an unusually early age – particularly for a girl with little formal education growing up in the cultural isolation of Nuoro, Sardinia.

Like many other apprentice writers, Deledda began her literary career by writing short stories and poems. She was soon to abandon her attempts at poetry, but even after gaining international fame with her many novels, she continued to explore the short-story form.

Her first stories appeared in local magazines and newspapers, and later on her association with the prestigious Roman journal *Nuova antologia* and the well-known newspaper *Corriere della sera* of Milan lasted from early in the twentieth century until her death in 1936. Her collected stories fill ten volumes.

Not every writer of fiction is equally adept at both the longer and shorter forms, but Deledda handles the novel's slowly unfolding plot, with its multiple sub-plots, as skilfully as the more immediate, concentrated character of the short story.

Deledda never veered from the Sardinian setting of her stories. Each one is built around a particular custom, belief, attitude, superstition, legend pertaining to Sardinian life at the turn of the century; they are the essence of her Sardinian experience, told with the mastery of a born storyteller. These stories also contain an emotional universality that charms as it reveals common human foibles, weaknesses and strengths. The supposedly senile grandfather in 'The Boy in Hiding' outfoxes his more sophisticated and headstrong sons without saying a word. The delinquent schoolboy in 'The Marten' is helpless to keep from stealing the dearest possession of a 'house nun'. These are stories of the sort of loneliness Valentina Lecis, the doctor's wife, felt, to her ultimate regret. And stories of deceit, as the young man in 'A Man and a Woman', who blindly accepts the time-honoured myth of the receptive older woman finds to his eventual humiliation.

Often at the core is an authentic but irrational fear of the unknown, such as in 'The Cursed House'. Sometimes the victims are in the end victors, but more often their ignorance or poverty seals an unjust fate. We enter into the psychology of a wide cast of characters belonging to a pre-industrial Sardinia that has now all but disappeared.

Introduction

What D. H. Lawrence said about Deledda's staying power in his introduction to the translation of her *'La madre'* ('The Mother') is even more true today, more than half a century later. Her stories and novels can still be read with interest, unlike those of many of her contemporaries. Perhaps the least part of that interest is an anthropological one, and acknowledging that does not in the least diminish the effectiveness and appreciation of her narrative powers.

As in all her fiction, Deledda's short stories are an integration of landscape and life. The harsh mountains and flowering valleys, the changing skies and empathetic weather all contrive to form a sympathetic chorus in the action, expressed with her characteristic blend of fantasy, myth and reality.

Deledda had the faculty of observing her cultural environment with a rare detachment even while she was part of it. She tells in her autobiographical novel, *Cosima,* how from an early age she listened to and absorbed the stories of servants and guests in her father's house. Later she was to collaborate with a magazine editor in Rome by providing articles about the folklore of her native region in central Sardinia. Her understanding of the world she depicted was both intellectual and visceral. She did not leave Sardinia until 1900, when she moved to Rome with her new husband. She returned to Sardinia infrequently, and never after 1911. But in her stories she returned again and again to paint the landscape and direct the characters she knew so well through their fateful, mythic dreams.

Translator's Note

Grazia Deledda often uses phrases and sayings that are a direct translation from the Sardinian language. Three Sardinian words have no equivalent in Italian or English, and I have left them untranslated. *A tanca* is a vast, enclosed stretch of pasture land for pigs, sheep, goats and cows. It was a sign of wealth and prestige to be the owner of a *tanca* – not to be confused with a mere sheepfold. The *bisaccia* is a kind of saddlebag, woven from wool, often with scenic decoration on its two large pockets at either end. It can be worn over the shoulders or slung over the horse's flanks. The third word, *focolare*, translates as 'fireplace'. It is not the usual fireplace with a chimney, but consists of four stones placed on the floor in the middle of the room for building the fire for cooking and heating. The smoke goes up through the cracks in the ceiling. Often a rack for smoking cheese is hung over it. Almost every little shack could have a *focolare*; only the well-to-do would have both a *focolare*, for cooking and curing cheese, and a fireplace in the kitchen.

The caps Deledda's countrymen wear are a variety of black stocking cap. The long wide tail can be folded forward to form a sun shield.

The Mistress and her Servants

A rosy aureola, arched and pure as a baby's lip, barely tinged the sky above the hill when Zia Austina Zatrillas got out of bed. Pale, tall and plump, with her hair gathered into a cap of red brocade, she resembled strong-armed, stern-faced Juno.

The rooster crowed a second time below in the courtyard encircled by a low wall of prickly pears, and the woman started at that second call, like St Peter in Pilate's atrium; but she was dressed by the rooster's third crow. The points of her bodice supported her full bosom, and a red jacket trimmed with blue roses repeated the pleats of her skirt. Each blouse sleeve was carefully and evenly puffed, and a silver belt squeezed her thick waist; the effect was as though she had given careful thought to each part of her attire.

'Well, then, what have you decided, Austì?' her

1

husband asked as he awoke and raised his dark, snub-nosed face from the pillow. 'What do you say? Do you mean to make me pay more rent for the sheepfold?'

'Yes, Daniele, my dear; I have to. Taxes have gone up, the servants want to be paid double.'

'My dear wife, remember that you've already raised my rent three times; besides, I've been your husband for thirty years and I'm tied here like a prisoner.'

'Taxes and expenses are going up, Danié! I'm going to raise your rent only fifty scudi, even though my cousin's willing to give me a hundred scudi more for the *tanca* than you give me.'

Her husband, confined to his bed by bad arthritis, grimaced in pain.

'All right, call the young servant for me; I'll send him to the fold to tell the shepherds to drive the herd from my *tanca* to yours. And let it be fifty scudi, Austì; but try to help me sell the pony for a good price. Last night I dreamed I had tamed him.'

'Don't worry. When haven't I looked after your interests?'

Touching her pocket to make sure that she had her keys, a thimble, a rosary and money, the woman went to wake up the maids she had locked in their room, particularly since the menservants were in town. She passed through the pantry, where stacks of white bread and barley bread seemed like striped columns of ivory and marble, and went into the large kitchen. It was Monday. The servants, who had spent most of the night drinking, were still asleep on mats around the *focolare*; streams of red light rained down from the holes in the low roof – holes made to let the smoke escape – illuminating the scene here and there. It looked like a bivouac; long blunderbusses and long knives in decorated and fringed sheaths, bridles and saddles, overcoats and capes of rough wool were hanging on the dark walls; wool *bisacce* striped like leopard skins, leather bags, cartridge boxes, powder horns, sheepskin over-jackets had been tossed casually on the floor; and in the dim light men were on the floor on their sides, on their backs, dressed in red and black, with oiled hair, woven knee socks, waists belted with strips of embroidered leather.

At the mere presence of their mistress they awoke immediately, and were on their feet in a second, ready for orders. The oldest looked like Amsicora, with a long curly white beard and still lively black eyes; the youngest looked like Aristeus, with black braids behind his ears, an olive complexion, red lips and blue-green eyes the colour of tamarisk leaves when they reflect the noon sky. The woman turned to him.

'Sadurru, my boy, go up to the old man.'

The servant stomped through the rooms and dark hallways loudly. At the master's doorway he encountered a young maid who came out hurriedly. Colliding, they cursed each other like two enemies.

'Boy,' the man said, his eyes burning like small flames, 'go to my sheepfold and tell the men to drive the herd from my *tanca* to my wife's. Help them and come back this evening. And don't poke the livestock or mistreat them because my wife has increased my rent.'

The young man said nothing; but when he arrived at the sheepfold he began to make fun of his employers.

'Those two are like two goat horns on the same head, and they treat each other like strangers.'

'Boy,' said the elderly servant, gathering up his skins and cork receptacles, 'you're a stranger. You've only been in the house for a few weeks and you think you can judge your employers.'

'You know the stories!'

'What do you know, monkey brains? Let one talk who has eaten their bread for thirty years. My mistress is a strong woman. At fifteen they made her marry that old sinner, and without her the family would have gone to ruin. She's the one who manages her own property and her husband's, she's the one who gives orders to the servants, and who says to them: "This roll of wool is mine and this is my husband's: don't mix them up." That way there is no quarrel; and their earnings are kept separate.'

'Because the master, they say, enjoyed himself when he was still strong, and would open the chest and take from the common pile to go to other women. And they say another curious thing. That the mistress loved another man. Diecu Delitala, from the time when she was a young girl; and that to avenge himself on the rival who took her away from him, this Diecu had a spell cast on the husband to make him fall out of love with his wife . . .'

The old servant was growing angry.

'Gossip! I don't know anything about it. I only know that my mistress has never looked at any man but her husband . . .'

'. . . And the master then walked in processions with the standard and cross, begging the saints to remove the spell. But a priest had done it and so it couldn't be undone; and so he grew old, in love with every woman except his wife. That's why he took his pleasures away from home.'

'All right, quiet, serpent's tongue; you eat their bread and shouldn't talk like that.' But the young servant laughed sneeringly, and his canine teeth shone like pearls.

While the shepherds completed the march across the green and gold *tanca* under the blue autumn sky, the master in his wooden bed, with a bottle on the table, dreamed of his ponies, and his wife worked along with her maidservants. The men had all left with their *bisacce* full of barley bread, some on horse-back, some on foot, others with a cart, some going towards the olive grove and others towards the moun-tain slope to plant the wheat. The house was large and the maids always had something to do. One poured the wheat into the millstone, another pour-ed off the oil; the youngest, with narrow waist and wide hips, went up and down, barefoot and agile, from the kitchen to the master's room, taking him food and drink and telling him what was going on in the world.

The mistress's calm presence was everywhere, her large black eyes downcast, the spindle and decorated distaff in her hands heavy with rings. She said little, was neither happy nor sad, and every once in a while received someone in the large kitchen that was like her throne room. Occasionally she would go up to her husband, and, without stopping her spinning, would ask his advice, or would open the chest to take money out or put it in.

Some women from Oliena came with skins of vinegar, vessels of must and rolls of rough wool. She gave them spun wool to weave for her, and for their linen she exchanged a *bisaccia* she had woven, with black palm trees and red and green flamingoes on a white background, like an oriental tapestry.

The priest who came every day to visit the sick man found the women in the courtyard and chatted with them a bit; then he went up to the old man. Little by little Zio Daniele's room filled up with people, old friends, and men who remembered the sick man because he was rich and had good wine. Among the others that day were two strangers come to buy a horse, and a man still young, robust, brown and taciturn.

The priest talked about Zia Austina, repeating verses from the Book of Proverbs.

'Who can find a virtuous woman? for her price is far above rubies.

'The heart of her husband doth safely trust in her, so that he shall have no need of spoil.

'She riseth also while it is yet night, and giveth

6

meat to her household, and a portion to her maidens.

'She considereth a field, and buyeth it: with the fruit of her hands she planteth a vineyard.

'She layeth her hands to the spindle, and her hands hold the distaff.

'She maketh herself coverings of tapestry; her clothing is silk and purple.

'She openeth her mouth with wisdom; and in her tongue is the law of kindness.'

The men listened, gathered around the young priest. From the little window they could see the hill covered by the sunset's rosy veil, and from that hill the sound of doves cooing and the odour of wild thyme wafted into the old man's room.

Diecu Delitala looked at the sick man and from time to time shook his head as though to chase away a fly. There he was, his old rival! What good had the spell done? The old man had been happy just the same, and now he lay on his bed like a just and powerful old king.

'What are you thinking about, Diecu Delità?' the old man asked, seeing he was so pensive.

Diecu Delitala straightened his cap on his strong dark head.

'Daniele Zatrì, these two men want to buy your yearling. Make a deal with them. But treat them like friends, if you can.'

The old man smiled maliciously. 'Go and see my wife.'

The three men went down to the kitchen and

found the woman sitting on a large throne-like chair, surrounded by her servants, who were cleaning the wheat.

'Austina Zatrì, these young men came to see about the yearling. How much do you want?'

'One hundred scudi.'

'Austina Zatrì! Not even if it were gold!'

'The pony is a nice sorrel. My brother offered me ninety-eight scudi for it.'

'Go on, treat us like friends of Diecu Delitala,' one of the young men said with emphasis.

The woman raised her serious eyes and looked at the three men; her eyes were sparkling but were cold and as distant as the stars.

When the priest met the three men in the street he began to tease Delitala.

'It's obvious that your friendship means nothing to her. She loves her husband . . .'

Diecu beat his fist against a wall: 'Father Farrà, that woman's heart is like stone.'

Meanwhile the shepherds travelled from one *tanca* to another and continued arguing about their employers.

'You've been their servant for thirty years and you should know about it,' Sadurru shouted. 'The young maid says that when you still had teeth you were in love with the mistress . . .'

'Every man who's met her has been in love with her and has wanted her. She's never noticed it, like a queen on her throne. Maybe she's noticed you,

8

monkey brains? Anyway, your feelings for her can be read on your sinful face. And tell that young maid to bite off her tongue and look for friends of her own kind. Does she confide in you when she lies down on your mat at night?'

'Exactly, when she lies down on my mat at night!'

'The devil take you both, you demons in disguise!'

The young servant snickered, and his teeth gleamed in the blood-red sunset. He seemed eager to quarrel and, among other things, said, 'Perhaps the woman was strong as long as she was young; but now that she is declining like the sun don't you think that, like the sun, she must lose her strength?'

Then the elderly servant threatened to tell their employers. 'You talk like their enemy; you aren't worthy to eat their bread. I'll have you run off!'

'Ha, ha, watch out I don't get you run off!'

Later the old man sat in front of the hut and swore under his breath. The young man had already left for town, and the shepherd felt sad like the evening, with a heavy heart and a bitter taste in his mouth.

'Now I can tell you, Juannepré,' he said to his companion, 'my mistress has only one fault: putting up with worthless people; but if I don't go back to town tonight and run off that no-good, I'll die from anger.'

'A king in the old days said: leave evening's anger till morning.'

And for a while the old man seemed calmer.

Between two oak trees loomed the horizon veiled in a luminous fog. In the background a deep blue in the distance like a strip of sea, then yellow like a beach, then red, violet, and azure. The new moon fell slowly, turning red as though attracted by the vaporous sunset; and everything around – the motionless and yet murmuring trees, the enormous boulders, the bushes – was covered by a golden-black veil giving everything a fantastic aspect. The oaks leaning over the cliffs seemed to have stopped there, surprised by the night, while they tried, one after the other, to reach the mountain peaks. And a mystery of shadows, of abysses, of unknown dangers, hid behind every rock in the woody slopes below. But until the sea-green, golden dawn arrived an infinite peace would reign, and plaintive, harmonious sounds would rise from the *tanca*. The tinkling of the flock gathered together in the enclosures blended with the last cricket song, with barking dogs, with a buzzing insect, with chirping birds seeming to greet each other from tree to tree before sleeping.

Suddenly the old shepherd stood up and said to his companion, 'I'm going. I have to go.'

And he walked a long way in the clear evening, across the silvery-black *tancas* under the silvery-blue autumn sky. An equivocal passion propelled him: love for his mistress, hate for the wicked servant; but also something he was unable to define, a strange discomfort such as he had once felt after a viper bite. The mysterious shadows and light that the autumn

10

evening spread over the solitary *tancas* passed into his heart.

But suddenly a north wind came up that seemed to extinguish the moon. Everything became black until a hill with reddish dots appeared in the distance. The shepherd quickened his steps, dragging his fatigue and his suspicions as he would drag sick and stubborn heifers. He was in front of the courtyard hedged by prickly pears; the house was dark, but over the low roof of the kitchen spread a yellowish light. He took off his big shoes, straightened his gaiters, and climbed up on the tree trunks supporting the woodpile, just as he climbed oak trees to cut tender branches for the animals. The wind blew angrily, sweeping the smoke from the roof; it was a night for lovers and thieves, and like a thief the servant leaned over the roof as far as the hole over the *focolare*.

Through a veil of smoke he saw the red fire below him, and his mistress and the young servant sitting next to the *focolare*. The woman was not spinning; like a queen at the foot of the throne, she was sitting on a stool next to a tall high-backed chair, and on it the distaff and spindle seemed bedded down next to each other like a married couple. The servant snickered and stared at the woman with his catlike eyes, telling her about the scene at the sheepfold in his own way.

'The old man seemed like a boar, he was so angry . . . I told him: how could someone not love

11

that woman just looking at her? Just knowing her goodness? Was it bad of me to talk that way?'

'You shouldn't talk about me ... in any way,' the woman said in a hard tone. 'I forbid you to ...'

'I can't help talking about you ... My own thoughts betray me ...'

'Ah, cursed bird, may you be shot dead!' swore the old man on the roof, and was about to spit on the head of the hypocrite. But the young man went on.

'I always think of you, and sometimes I even say something bad about you just to be able to talk about you ... I like to hear the others praise you; and that's what happened today. You can send me away; I'll be a homeless vagabond, but I'll be thinking of you ... And you ... you ... what will you do for me?'

She stretched her hands out before the fire and trembled all over, as though from a chill.

'I won't send you away,' she said in a slightly hoarse voice. 'If we send people away who love us, then who can we stay with?'

'She spoke like that to me, too – to me, too ... once ...' thought the old man on the roof. And looking down the hole he seemed to see all his past ... He was there, in the place of the young servant; but she had never come down off her chair, and while talking to him had never put down her spindle, just as a queen never puts down her sceptre ...

Other times, other men. He, for example, would

12

never have dared to put his stool next to hers like that impudent one was now doing . . . And she . . . she had never let anyone take her hand like that damned stranger was doing.

The old man scratched on the roof to warn the woman that someone was watching her; but the wind covered every sound, and those two down there were listening only to their own passion.

'Austì, Austì,' the young servant said, coming ever closer to her, 'you are right not to send me away. I'll be your real husband; and the old man will die and leave you in peace once and for all . . . If you don't want to marry me before a priest it doesn't matter; but I'll be your real husband . . .'

And the woman let him talk and act. Just one moment more and something terrible – for the old man up there – would happen; but he felt crushed by an enormous weight, as if all the world had collapsed upon him, and he felt he was already dead and staring into hell.

What could he do, anyway? Give a shout? She would have hated him for ever. Go down and knock on the door? He would postpone the terrible experience until another day, another hour. The boy's wicked words came back to mind.

'She was strong as long as she was young, but now that she is declining like the sun . . .'

At once he slid down into the courtyard and pounded furiously on the door. The woman opened it herself, a little paler than usual, but calm and impassive.

13

The old man leapt over to the *focolare* and grabbed the young man by the hair, as though to hold him still and make him listen to his accusations.

'Austina Zatrillas, look him in the face! He is your worst enemy. He wants to dishonour and ruin you. He goes around the *tanca* saying that you are about to become his lover. Look at him closely! He brags that you'll poison your husband so you can marry him . . . He's your maid's lover and both of them are plotting against you! Look at him closely . . .'

She looked at him, but her face revealed only a slight fear. Without speaking she came up to the two servants to separate them, but the young man, who hadn't spoken and whose face had become black, as though suddenly rotten and putrefied, drew out his jackknife, opened it, jumped up from a hunched position and caused the old man to fall backwards.

She shouted, 'Hurry, everyone, quickly . . .'

The old man was propped against the wall looking at the blood that seemed to gush from his red jacket, spreading over his belt. The young man, his hair in his face, picked up his cap and hurled himself towards the door shouting, 'He asked for it . . . you are my witness . . . he asked for it.'

He went out leaving the door open. His footsteps could be heard through the loud wind.

Then the woman ran to open the inside door to the maids who had leapt from their beds, while the old man fell slowly into a sitting position, his back

14

against the wall. His head was nodding like he was agreeing, yes, yes. 'Yes, I asked for it . . .' he seemed to be saying . . .

A Man and a Woman

The rumour got around, who knows how – the way
all rumours get started – that the old woman gave
money to young men.

They were even talking about it on that autumn
evening as far away as the road-keeper's house at
Santa Marga, eight kilometres from where the
woman lived. It's true, however, that all the gossip
from round about came and left the road-keeper's
house like mice that travel in cargo ships, in the carts
carrying coal and holm-oak bark to the ports, and in
public carriages, or simply on the travellers' horses.

The road-keeper's wife ran a kind of canteen. All
the passers-by stopped there, where they could also
play cards. And that very evening two men were playing and talking about the old woman who gave
money to young men.

'And if she gives it away it means she has it. She'll

16

lend it or give it away to charity,' observed Comare Marga (as they called the road-keeper's wife, even though it wasn't her real name). 'If I had money to give away, I'd give it to young men and not to old men. If old people at the tannery still need money it means they haven't been good at anything. The young need help.'

The two laughed into their cards. This Comare Marga, huddled up there in the doorway, with her shabby dress of black wool that time and soil had nearly reduced to its original state of fleece, was really still like an innocent lamb: she didn't know anything about men or the world.

'Well, then, Comare Marga, now that you are old you can help me because I'm young. Give me at least sixty scudi so I can go to America and make my fortune. Come on, out with sixty scudi.'

But an abrupt kick under the table from his companion made him look up; in the opposite corner of the little room he saw the son of Comare Marga and the road-keeper stretched out on a whitish reed mat in the shadows, wearing an old pair of blue trousers and a peaked cap.

Though it was early evening Comare Marga's son was sleeping, as he always slept, even during the day, when not obliged to help his father. He was sleeping, but he was a boy who even in his sleep would not allow offence or permit anyone else to offend his most distant relative.

Therefore, the two men finished their game, continuing to talk among themselves without maligning

Comare Marga any further. Besides, she was also napping and roused herself only to take their money. which she put in a pot above the high chimney cowl as soon as the customers left.

Then her son's eyes of black crystal shone, opening and soon closing again, in the shadowy corner. He raised and immediately lowered his head, murmuring as in a dream, 'It's time to put an end to this story.'

His mother paid little attention to him, as she often heard him grumble in his sleep. She left the door open and went to bed in the little adjoining room, next to her husband who was also asleep and snoring. From the way he was snoring you could tell he was dog tired.

In the other room her son opened his eyes again, moved his hands and crossed them on his chest. He was alone. He watched a log burning down in the fireplace in the middle of the dark, shadowy room, the embers falling like petals from a red flower. From the crack in the door he smelled the night air, a mixture of stable odours and fresh grass. And he heard an ox chewing nearby and the murmur of water far away.

In his half-awake state he had heard everything that the men had said, and he was ruminating on it now, like the ox chewing the grass outside in the dark shed, while sleep was still rocking him with that distant watery voice in the mild autumn night. He could still hear the flat warm voice of the younger man.

18

'That young fellow from Sorgono, the one staying with the other masons building the house, told me about it. The house is for the woman. She's married for the second time. Her first husband was old and rich and she was young and poor. That husband was as jealous as a dog, and stingy, and he kept her locked up and nearly starving for twenty years. When he died she married a poor young man, she almost an old woman. But this young man wasn't enough for her and she immediately began to take other lovers. Her husband beat her and what did she do? She kicked him out of the house and because he kept on bothering her and threatening to kill her, she moved away and came to live in our town. She opened a draper's shop and started building the house. Well, while this house was being built she went to see it every day this past summer; she looked at the house, but also at the masons, the youngest ones, and they fell for her, one after the other, from the height of the scaffolding like fruit from a tree! Gossips say that the house cost a lot of gold. The nice thing is that the older she gets the more she likes young men; to hell with mortal sin! Now she lives in this new house with an iron balcony all around it decorated with gilded apples, and her shop off the piazza is like those in big cities. Her name, Onofria Dau, is on the outside on an iron plaque like the one over Christ on the cross.'

Suddenly he got up, lit a candle, and looked inside the pot over the fireplace, bending over to see the bottom, smelling the money like it was something to eat. And the copper coins really seemed like cooked beans, with a scattering of silver coins looking like fresh beans.

He stood there a while, suspended and motionless, counting the money with his eyes. Then, as though removing the pot from the fire, he took it by the handle and opened the door with his foot. He went as far as the meadow and, kneeling down, poured the money into a handkerchief he had taken from his pocket. Folding and knotting the corners of the handkerchief tightly, he set off.

The parcel in his hands was hard and heavy like an iron ball. He walked along the clear wide road between dark meadows, under the little golden points of the Big Dipper. The town was over there; he seemed to see a cross on the vaporous, black horizon sprinkled with stars: a cross with a plaque over it saying: Onofria Dau.

The distant sound of water, the nibbling of a grazing horse, the odour of damp grass at night accompanied him on his journey.

'If it's true, it's true,' he was thinking. 'Now it's probably eight-thirty, and at the rate I'm going I'll be there by ten. I'll take twenty scudi, ah, not a centesimo less, and then I'll go straight to the port and get on a boat. I'll go any place in the world, to Corsica or Africa, but I don't want to stay here any longer. I don't want to be a road-keeper, spreading gravel on the road all day so others can travel on it and change horses at the coach house, and I always there, always stuck there like a donkey going around the millstone. My father can do that as long as he wants, but not me. And if my plan doesn't work I'll come back and put the money back in the pot. Get there in good time, Ghisparru Loddo; keep walking.'

He kept walking; he made big plans and felt almost happy tossing the package from hand to hand like it was an orange. If the thing didn't work out he wouldn't have touched a soldo; all the money back in the pot again on his return, within three hours. On the other hand, if everything went well, as soon as he arrived at the unknown point towards which he was moving, he would write to his mother, apologizing and sending her the first money he earned.

Deep down, however, he was fully aware of what he wanted to do and he knew why he had to do it. He knew very well that he was lazy and that his father had no hope for him. But he was trying to justify himself to himself.

'You're a lazy lout and have to change your life; you have to go where there is work suitable for you, Ghisparru Loddo. Get going.'

He walked on. There was no way to get lost: one step after another towards his goal, just as life is one step after another towards death. As the kilometres went by, the line of the rocky hills above the town became sharper, a sombre black against the liquid black of the horizon. He believed he even saw, at the end of the road, the woman's house with the iron balcony all around.

But as he came closer he had some doubts about the success of his undertaking. He began to think about the woman whom he didn't know: fat, robust, with her great bodice-laced breasts drooping towards her stomach. Her black eyes a little stern, a moustache over her fat, protruding lip; in other words, an elderly, well-to-do woman, like many he had known, like he had seen the last Sunday of September at the Feast of Sant'Elia – women who still love to have a good time even if they don't show it. Women who basically aren't displeasing to men. At least he didn't mind them; or, to tell the truth, he didn't like or dislike them, because all women, to think about it, were the same to him, whether ugly or beautiful, old or young.

He entered the deserted town. A dog barked in the deep silence; a light shone from a small ground-floor window; he looked in as he passed and saw a sick woman on a wooden bed and a little girl sitting up with her.

He didn't know why his thoughts changed mood: as he walked along he was feeling a little lost, as if, after that scene he had just witnessed, the darkness ahead of him had grown denser.

In fact, other windows and doors lighted up the street from time to time until the point where it widened into the piazza, so that once there he could clearly distinguish the house of Onofria Dau. It was there, in front of him, with the hills in the background, greyish, with a necklace of gilded apples on the balcony; it was there, closed, silent and still as reality.

He felt his heart pound with anxiety. He seemed

22

to have reached the source of a river, swimming against the current; and though he was also strong and sure, determined to win, the current beat against him furiously, and in the depths of his heart he trembled with fear.

Then he crossed the piazza and knocked on Onofria Dau's door, under the sign. From the men's talk he knew that the woman, to better do as she liked, did not even have a servant: he was certain, therefore, that the dark figure on the balcony asking who he was and what he wanted was she.

'I'm Ghisparru Loddo, son of the road-keeper at Santa Marga. Open the door. I need to buy a wool blanket urgently because my mother has pneumonia.'

The improvised, childish lie made him want to laugh, but he became serious when he saw the figure go back in and heard her footsteps inside the house.

'It cannot be true that she lives alone,' he thought. 'She wouldn't open the door so readily. Someone could even kill her. I could kill her and rob her, just like Doctor Lecis's sister-in-law was killed and robbed the other night.'

Again he felt his heart pounding, and a muddle of fierce thoughts tangled in his mind: a light sweat dampened the palms of his hands. But as soon as the door opened and a tall, beautiful woman appeared, with a clear white Madonna's face surrounded by the black halo of a veil, with blue, almond-shaped eyes reflecting the flame of the candle she held in her hand, he felt his evil terror flee with the surrounding shadows. He knew immediately that he wouldn't kill and he wouldn't sell himself.

He didn't even dare ask the woman if she was Onofria Dau. He saw only that the entry floor was white and shining like her face, and he stamped his feet on the threshhold so that no dust from the road he had travelled would be carried inside.

The woman moved away without speaking; when she reached the door to the shop, at the foot of the stairs at the end of the entry hall, she handed the candle to Ghisparru.

'I don't carry it inside because it wouldn't take anything to start a fire. Stay here, please. I'll go and get the blanket.'

He stood there with the candle in one hand and his package in the other; from the open door came the odour of new linen and perfumed soap, and he watched her step nimbly on a chair and pull down a blue package from the shelf. Then he watched her climb back down, unwrap the package at the counter and bring out a yellowish blanket with red stripes.

'See if this is all right. Put the candle on the stairs. How did your mother get this pneumonia? The weather is still warm.'

'Oh, just like sicknesses come on,' he said gravely, looking at the blanket, convinced that his mother, sick in bed, needed it to get rid of her pneumonia.

The woman unfolded the blanket, holding her arms wide so he could see it better; and she looked into his eyes to see if he was satisfied; and he had the impression that she smiled at him, with her white, strong teeth between red lips; that she looked at him and smiled to please him.

'Touch it, feel it, it's fine wool. Put the candle down.'

He placed it and the parcel on the third step of the stairs, and, taking the blanket by the hem, he felt it, and then silently helped refold it.

On the wall his shadow and the woman's imitated their actions grotesquely.

'Is it all right, then?'

'It's fine. How much is it?'

'It would be twenty-two lire, but, considering the circumstances, I'll give it to you for twenty. Have you called a doctor? I'll rewrap it for you now.'

Her last words came from inside the shop: she had already deftly put the blanket back in the blue wrapper on the counter. The man picked up his parcel; when he leaned over it seemed to him that all his blood ran to his head. The dizzy sensation was followed by dark rage; he didn't want to be played with like that; he didn't want so stupidly to lose the money his mother had earned coin by coin; he had promised himself not to waste it. No, by God, he wouldn't waste it. Then he felt miserable. It seemed like he was betrayed by fate, by the woman who was not old and didn't buy men (she sold them her smile instead), by the men who slandered her; and finally he was seized by the desire to fling himself on her, to grab her, or at least to hit her with his package. But as soon as he entered the shop he saw a man – undoubtedly a servant – lying against the wall between the exit and the counter. Like a thief he went out immediately. Fear cooled his rage. He wanted to run away, to save his money, but his fear was then conquered by shame. The woman was again standing before him, handing him the blue package.

Then he wanted at least to protect what was his by rights, and even more, if possible.

'Give it to me for twelve lire; it's not worth any more.' (He was immediately sorry he hadn't said ten.)

She frowned at him, suddenly becoming old.

'You're crazy, my boy; give you a blanket for twelve lire that cost me twenty?'

He looked her straight in the eye, up close, separated only by the wall of their parcels; yes, she was old. And now he tried to smile at her, to flatter her with his eyes; and suddenly he remembered his evil plans.

'If you can, fine, Onofria Dau, if not, never mind. I'm sorry to have bothered you at this hour . . . but they told me . . . they told me . . .'

He gazed resolutely into her eyes, wanting his face to suggest his thoughts to her. He had no more shame, nor fear of the man in there: it was enough that Onofria should understand.

But Onofria didn't understand or didn't want to. She knew only that she must sell her blanket and be satisfied with an honest profit. She bowed her head thoughtfully, until her cheek was resting on the package, and she tried a last wheedling look, but without hope.

'Give me at least sixteen lire. Believe me, I'm losing four lire, but since you came at this hour, for your sick mother . . . go on, take it!'

'I can't,' he said moving away; and he seemed to be saving himself and his parcel; but she followed him with her package, trying to force it into his arms.

'All right, then; take it at your price, since it's for your sick mother.'

He wanted to shout, but didn't for fear of the man inside. After all, he wasn't throwing his mother's money away; a wool blanket is always a wool blanket.

And so he kneeled down on the white marble floor, just like he had kneeled down on the dark grass in the meadow, and untied his parcel, picking out the silver coins: there were exactly twelve. He angrily put them into her cupped hand without looking at her. She put the package down on the floor also, in order to count her money, while he put away his handkerchief.

Chiaroscuro

The man was handsome – tall, slender, with a brown, predatory face like a young Arab – and he seemed as open and honest as his past was obscure and questionable. But when he talked about the vicissitudes of his life they took on an almost romantic flavour. He sat on the stool that his tiny landlady had hurriedly put outside the door as soon as he appeared at the other end of the moonlit piazza. With his nervous arms crossed on his chest, his right leg twisted around his left, he would talk. Once in a while he would turn towards the wall to spit, and raise his dark face so that his white teeth and the whites of his large black eyes shone even in the half light. His voice was full of scorn. He addressed the woman huddled on the doorstep listening to him religiously, but he raised his voice to be heard also by the neighbours who were leaning here and there against the empty white lime carts, or grouped in the middle of the piazza, with a mountain looming in the background that seemed made of marble.

But the neighbours no longer paid attention to him (having heard his story so many times), and they preferred to gather around Sidore, the little mason who also owned a lime furnace and gave them work delivering his goods.

'What do you think, Sabé,' the stranger was saying, 'that my family is just any kind of family? It's probably the best in my town. Go and ask around if you don't believe me. My father has property and money; he's so rich and independent that he doesn't even have to greet the bishop if he doesn't want to. And my mother? She is fair and beautiful. She never raises her voice, and all the women go to her for advice. She knows how to write, too, even though she is old-fashioned. My brothers have all married rich women. We have a courtyard as big as this piazza, all covered with a pergola; it's so nice and cool that it feels like a cloudy day in May – not to mention all the things that are inside the house. In my estimation the stuff my mother gives to the poor is worth more than your mayor owns.'

Sabera, in spite of her admiration for her tenant, tried to defend the undisputed wealth of the mayor.

'What are you talking about, Caralu? As far as I'm concerned there's no place in the world where people are rich enough to give away to charity what Don Giame possesses!'

But Caralu had also been to other parts of the world.

'Be quiet, silly woman! What do you know? Because you own a shack and a waterless well do you think you can judge what others have? The smartest devil in the world isn't clever enough to guess how much money my father has. It's true there's money in America, but things are expensive and you spend more than you have. What good is that? In my house there are heaps of provisions, and my father puts money aside. That is true wealth. And so my father is respected like a king. In the evening he sits on the bench under the pergola with my mother beside him, and my sisters-in-law, the children, the servants all around him – not even a Royal Court could do any better! Well, then, as I was telling you, my ruin came from wanting to marry a poor girl. She was tall, goodlooking, and plump, however – enough to console any man!'

Skinny little Sabera tried to object.

'All the women in your town are black as the damned in hell.'

'Be quiet, dirty beggar! My fiancée was fair and beautiful. She lived alone, like you, but her house was out of the way, and had a low window without bars. One night I was leaning against this window, like this, at my leisure. Suddenly the shutter gave way and I fell inside. The girl was in bed. She said she screamed, but I didn't notice. Besides if she had really screamed someone would have heard. Anyway, I said, "If you want to, I'll marry you tomorrow" . . .

She went to the judge and brought charges against me. She said I had pushed my way through the window, gagged her with a handkerchief, and so on. Then she dropped her complaint, because she didn't want to ruin me, she said. She even paid the expenses, two hundred beautiful lire like two hundred angels from heaven. I said to my father: "Let's pay these expenses." But my father answered: "Then everyone will say you are at fault; that won't look good!" My mother asked me: "Are you guilty or not? If you say yes we are ready to pay." I said no, what the devil? Because, think about it, Sabera, if I had behaved like the girl said, would she have dropped the charges and paid the expenses?'

The landlady sighed. 'If she loved you! . . . A woman is always a woman . . .'

'Damn all women! You know what I think? A man works all week for a woman, and it was God who started it: He created the world and made man just for woman! And so after that happened, I said: "Damn all women!" And I went to America. I left without a penny in my pocket, you know, like an emigrant, because my father wouldn't give me a cent, and I'd rather hang myself than steal from my own house and make my mother unhappy. I went to work on the Panama Canal. What terrible times, my dear! I had to live in a shack with three other men from my town, three desperate men who kept their money in a sack like beggars. There were three little sacks inside one big one: seven hundred lire all together. Every once in a while those three beggars counted their money, and when they went far away to work one of them would stay to guard that treasure of the King of Spain! It made me laugh to remember that once my mother had a thousand-lire note and she thought it was a fifty. One day I had a fever – that illness that still bothers me – and they left me alone in the shack. They went somewhere far away, I don't know where, maybe to hell. I felt better and went back to work. Was I supposed to rot in there just to guard their treasure? Fact is, on that day I had a fight with the foreman, and not being a man to take humiliation, I quit it all there and then and left. I went to Brazil, where I hoped to find work. In the meantime, do you know what those three beggars did? They telegraphed my father saying I had taken their sack of money! He promised to pay, provided that I agreed. Imagine me agreeing to that! I was sick; otherwise I would have gone after those three and plucked them like chickens. I went back to my town half dead and I can't tell you the troubles I had because of this business!

'My mother, with her heart of gold, said: "Those poor men have reason to be angry with you, my son; if you hadn't left the shack the thieves wouldn't have taken the sack. So let's give them the money!" But my father said: "If we give them money it's like confessing that Caralu is guilty. Are you or not?"

'I said, "No, no, no."

'Finally I couldn't take it any more, and I went away again. I'll never go back to my town: it's a hellish place. Now I'm here and doing well. I'm peaceful, respected, I have a good job; if I wanted I could marry the best girl in town . . . What more could I want?'

Sabera listened, pale, motionless, fixing her large melancholy eyes on him. No, he wasn't lying . . . Only, she still didn't know exactly what his good job was. He would leave early in the morning, come back at noon, go out again, come back late in the evening and often spend the night away from home. He ate only once a day, was frugal, didn't drink. Sabera, who for a long time had been the maid of an old ex-marshal, from whom she had inherited her small house and furniture, tried to make the voluntary exile of her young lodger less unhappy. She ironed his shirts and suits, and every evening she waited for him on the doorstep, without deigning to respond to the jokes and the coarse allusions of her neighbours. Three of these, the carpenter, the blacksmith, and the mason, had courted her for several years. From the first two, very poor, whose devotion may have been a little calculated (the poor are always suspect!) Sabera had removed every hope. As for the third she was unsure: he was ugly, but he was nearly wealthy.

When her lodger was late coming home, little Sidore, white with lime up to his hair, with his jacket over his shoulders, would lean against the wall next to the woman and say in a low voice, 'There's no use waiting for him! He's at the Milese's playing cards with Don Giame. Listen to me, little woman; get up and let's go inside . . . Let the priest take care of the rest.'

And he would bring out a fistful of nuts from his pocket, or a pomegranate, and give them to her. She would take the present, but would not grant his desires.

One evening he came over while Caralu was rocking back and forth on her stool.

'I went to your town, you know! I sold your mother two cartloads of lime. Guess who I also sold a sack to? To that tall girl who was supposed to marry you. She has to plaster her house because she's going to get married, to a certain Muschineddu who has come back from America – a short, dark . . .'

Caralu jumped to his feet, stiff and livid; but suddenly he sat down again and began to laugh: a nervous laugh, a sob with no end.

'And that means she has taken the leap!' he finally shouted. 'She did it with me, now I can say it! But men who go to America become like foreigners; they don't care if the woman they marry is virtuous or not!'

The two didn't answer immediately, but after a moment the mason, in order to vindicate himself, said slyly, 'Muschineddu is one of your American friends?'

'Which friends?' Caralu asked contemptuously. 'I've never had labourers or farmhands for friends.'

'Those with the sack!'

'Oh, you all go to hell, rabble!' he said, getting up and going to his little room, where he remained writing into the night.

During the next few days every time he returned

to the house he asked if there was any mail for him. He was agitated, feverish, and as the letter did not arrive, he finally took to insulting his landlady.

'It arrived, you opened it and tore it up . . .'

'Oh, I don't deserve this! I'm not like the other women you've known . . .'

Then he slapped her. 'To teach you better manners! I'm going now and I'll never set foot in this house again.'

'At least pay me the rent! You haven't paid for four months . . . And you treat me like this . . .' the woman cried, with her arm over her head for fear of getting hit again.

He took out his wallet of yellow leather stamped with the head of Cavallotti (the work of an artist from Dorgali), but then thought better of it and put it back in his pocket.

'I'll pay you when I feel like it!'

He went away and was gone for two days. In the meantime the letter he was waiting for arrived, which Sabera didn't hesitate to hold over the steaming coffee pot and open without tearing. It was from Caralu's mother.

Dear son, it is pointless and dangerous for you to return. The girl has decided to marry Muschineddu.

She says she has forgiven you long ago, but she doesn't want to hear anything more about you, especially since her new fiancé is convinced you took the sack from the shack in Panama. Also, he has threatened to kill you if you come back here. As for your father, he insists you keep out of town, otherwise he'll call the notary immediately and make a will disinheriting you. Dear son, you have always been respectful towards your parents: therefore, be obedient and don't bring more unhappiness to your mother. If you continue to live far from here, you will see that you will no longer be slandered. We will think about finding you a serious and well-to-do wife as soon as you have settled down. With this hope I send you my love and at the end of the week I'll send you your usual monthly allowance. Your mother.

Sabera resealed the envelope with saliva and ironed it flat. Now she understood many things, and she regretted not having opened her lodger's letters before, and she was sorry that she had given him such faith and respect.

'Have you seen that rascal?' she asked little Sidore when he leaned against the wall next to her door.

'He's at the Milese's playing cards. His face is as black as gunpowder and says he has a fever.'

'Do me a favour and take this letter to him. Did you know he doesn't stay here any more? I don't ever want to see him again . . .'

'Good! And so you'll make a decision. What do you think, Sabé? I'll modernize your house, replace the broken floor tiles, rebuild the stairway . . . What do you think, Sabé?'

'Tonight I have a headache; I'm very angry. Tomorrow night I'll give you a definite answer.'

He kept insisting. She repeated: 'Tomorrow, tomorrow.'

The next day Caralu returned. He had a fever and went to bed, grinding his teeth and punching at some invisible thing; but from time to time he would reread his mother's letter and calm down.

Sabera bent over his burning face. 'Eat something, my dear, be quiet, it will all pass . . .'

He looked at her with astonishment, almost as though he saw her for the first time, but he refused the food and was silent. When she went away he felt like he was suffocating in prison. What misery in that little room with the whitewashed cane ceiling! Through the window, beyond the courtyard wall studded with pieces of glass, he could see a grey landscape sadder than winter: rocks the shape of frogs and enormous turtles clambered over the wild slope; the shrubs and hedges were the same dull grey.

Suddenly Sabera heard her lodger raving and calling to her in a stifled voice. Trembling, she ran to him and he grabbed her like a drowning man.

'I'm dying . . . I'm dying . . . it's even too late to call the priest . . . Sabera, you are a good person: as soon as I die start walking to my father . . . tell him . . . yes, that I threw myself out of the window, that he should at least pay my expenses . . . And also the sack, I took it. Tell him he should give everything back to those beggars! I didn't tell him the truth when he asked me, because I didn't want . . . I didn't

37

want to make my mother unhappy... Or for her, for her to know...'

While he clung to her wrists and seemed to want to pull her down with him into the kingdom of shadows, Sabera began to cry like a baby. Her tears fell on the sick man's face.

'I'll go... I'll go... And if your father won't pay I will... But be quiet, die peacefully...'

Little by little he calmed down; his breathing became easier, and his hands, damp with cold sweat, relaxed. His fever broke and he slept peacefully, but Sabera watched over him all night long.

In the piazza the neighbours were laughing as they listened to Sidore tell them a spicy story. He had seen the lodger return and was not surprised that Sabera didn't appear; so he was speaking badly about women, telling anecdotes that did them little honour.

'Because, you see, take an honest man and a criminal and put them in front of a woman. If she's blindfolded she might choose the honest man by mistake, but if she can see she'll always take the other one. Once, a woman I knew...'

He raised his voice so she could hear, just as Caralu used to do; but Sabera kept her vigil in the little room where her lodger slept, handsome and peaceful as a little boy; and outside everything was silent under the light of the moon that made the rocky distance blue and the glass shards on the crumbling wall shine like diamonds...

The Fawn

'At one time,' Malafazza, Baldassarre Mulas's servant, was saying to the cattle dealer who had come to Mulas's sheepfold to buy some heiffers, 'my master was, you might say, a gentleman. He lived in that big house with the iron balcony next to the church of San Baldassarre, and his wife and daughter had skirts of pure wool and embroidered shawls like ladies. Of course the young girl had to marry a nobleman, a rich man so God-fearing he wouldn't open his mouth to keep from sinning. But the day before the wedding the master's wife – still a young, pretty woman – was seen kissing a twenty-year-old soldier on leave, behind the church.'

'Ohi, what a scandal! There's never been one like it.'

'The girl was jilted and died of a broken heart. Then my master began to spend weeks and months and whole seasons in the sheepfold, without ever going back to town. He almost never speaks, but he's good – even stupid, to tell the truth! Dogs, the cat, beasts are his friends! He even gets on with deer! Now he's made friends with a fawn; someone probably took her newborns and in desperation she came this far looking for them. My master is so quiet that the animal comes near him; but when she sees me she runs like the wind. She's got the right idea; if I can I'll take her alive and sell her to a hunter. But here's my master . . .'

Baldassarre Mulas was coming across the green clearing, wearing a hood on his head and a large white beard like a little dwarf of the woods. At his call the nice fat cows and the red, still wild heiffers came up meekly, letting their flanks be patted, and their mouths opened; and the terrible dog wagged his tail as though he recognized a friend in the dealer.

However, the business couldn't be concluded. Although the servant Malafazza, a dirty rascal and dark as a Bedouin, had portrayed his master as stupid, the latter showed he knew his business by not budging from the price first asked; and the dealer had to go away empty-handed.

The servant, who was returning to town as he did every evening, walked with him for a while and from afar his master saw them gesturing and laughing. Perhaps they were making fun of him; but by now the opinions of others were not important to him. Left alone, he returned to his cabin, put a bowl of milk on the grassy clearing, and sitting on a rock began to cut up a marten skin.

All around the vast clearing, green with new autumn grass, there was a biblical peace: the rosy sun was falling behind the violet high plain of Goceano, the rosy moon was rising from the violet woods around Nuoro. The herd grazed peacefully, and the heiffers' fur shone red in the sunset; the silence was such that distant sounds seemed to be coming from underground. A dignified-looking man, dressed in fustian but wearing a Sardinian cap, passed by the cabin leading two reddish oxen dragging an ancient silver ploughshare turned upwards. He was a poor gentleman who did not disdain to plough and sow his land. He greeted old Baldassarre without stopping.

'Well, have you seen your beloved today?'

'It's still early. If she isn't hungry she doesn't show up, that little devil.'

'What are you making with that skin?'

'Shoe laces. I've discovered that marten skin is more waterproof than dog skin.'

'It's rain resistant. Strange! Well, God be with you.'

'And may you go with Mary.'

After the man had disappeared with his plough shining like a silver cross all was silent once again; but as the sun continued to set, the old man looked somewhat uneasily towards the line of scrub behind the clearing, and finally quit his work and sat still. The cows had gathered into herds, first turning as though to look at the sun suspended on the horizon: red and blue vapours rose and, lightly veiled, everything seemed to throb with sadness: the blades of grass moving even without wind gave the impression of eyelids blinking over eyes ready to weep.

The old man kept looking at the bushes behind the clearing. It was about this time that the fawn came near the cabin. The first day he had seen her jump out of the bushes, frightened as though she were pursued by hunters. She had stopped a moment to look around with her large eyes sweet and brown as a child's, then swiftly and silently she disappeared again, as though flying across the clearing. She was blonde, with hoofs like polished wood, grey horns as delicate as branches of dry asphodel.

The second day she stayed just a little longer. The fawn saw the old man, looked at him, and fled. He would never forget that look that had something human about it – imploring, tender and suspicious at the same time. At night he dreamed about the fawn that was fleeing across the clearing: he would follow it, manage to grab it by its back hoofs and hold it, panting and shy, in his arms. Not even a sick little lamb, or a calf condemned to the slaughter house, never a wounded marten or a hare in the nest had made him feel that all-consuming tenderness. The throb of the little beast spoke to his heart; he would return to his solitary cabin with her and no longer feel alone in the world, taunted and ridiculed even by his servant.

But unfortunately it did not happen like that in reality. The fawn came a little nearer every day, but as soon as she saw the servant or some other person,

or if the old man made a move, she took off like a
low-flying bird, barely leaving a silver furrow among
the reeds beyond the clearing. When the old man
was alone and motionless on his rock stool, however,
she would linger, suspicious as always, nibbling the
grass, but every once in a while lifting her delicate
little head; she would start at every sound, turn
rapidly here and there, jump into the bushes. Then
she would return, come close, look at the old man.

Those eyes melted the shepherd with tenderness.
He smiled at her silently, like god Pan must have
smiled at the fawns in mythological forests. And as
though she too were fascinated by that smile, the
little beast would come closer, graceful and light on
her slender legs, lowering her head from time to
time as though to sniff the treacherous ground.

The milk and pieces of bread that the old man
placed at a certain distance drew her. One day she
took a little piece of ricotta cheese and fled; on
another day she came as far as the bowl, but as soon
as she had touched the milk with her tongue she
started, jumped on her four legs as if the ground
were burning her and ran. Immediately afterwards
she returned. Then the races and returns were more
frequent, less shy, almost coquettish. She would jump
high, turn around as though trying to catch her tail
with her teeth; she would scratch her ear with her
hoof, look at the old man, and he got the impression
that she too was less sad and frightened and that she
was smiling at him.

One day he put the bowl a few steps from his rock,

almost by the cabin door, chasing away the cat who expected to take advantage of the milk. A little later the fawn came up calmly, drank the milk, looked inside curiously. He watched motionless, but when he saw her so near, sleek, palpitating, he was overcome by the desire to touch her, and he stretched out his hand. She jumped on her four little hoofs, her snout dripping milk, and ran; but she returned and he didn't try to touch her again.

But by now he knew her and was certain that she would end by staying with him voluntarily. No animal is milder or more sociable than a fawn. As a boy he had had one that followed him everywhere and slept next to him at night.

To better attract his new friend and keep her with him all day without using force, he thought to go in search of a nest of fawns, to take one from it and tie it inside the cabin. In that way the other one, seeing a companion, would be more easily tamed. But as much as he went around looking, it wasn't an easy matter. One had to go towards the mountains, to the slopes of Gonare to find fawns; and he wasn't used to hunting. He only found a crow with a broken wing, laboriously flapping the other one in a vain attempt to fly. He took it and mended it, holding it against his chest; but when the fawn saw him with the big bird she fled without coming closer. She was jealous. Then the old man hid the crow behind the herd. The servant found it there and took it to town to some boys he knew, and when the master complained about it, he said, 'If you don't keep quiet,

44

I'll catch the fawn and sell her to some unsuccessful hunter.'

'If you touch her, I'll break your ribs, as true as the true cross is!'

'You? What are you good at?' said the rascal laughing. 'Eating bread and honey!'

But that day, after the departure of the dealer and servant, the old man waited for the fawn in vain. Shadows fell and not even the rustle of the wind interrupted the silence of the hazy evening. The old man became sad. He didn't doubt for an instant that the servant had caught the animal and had taken it to town.

'You must have let yourself get caught! If only you had stayed with me!' he grumbled, sitting in front of the fire in his cabin, while the cat, impervious to his master's sorrow, licked the milk from the bowl. 'By now they will have tied you up and quartered you. This also was your destiny . . .'

And all his bitterest memories returned to him; they returned horrible and deformed as cadavers tossed up by the sea.

The next day and the days after that he began to quarrel with the servant, forcing him to quit.

'Go, may you break your legs like you broke the poor fawn's.'

Malafazza sniggered. 'Yes, I broke them! I caught her. I cut off her hocks and I took her to a hunter. I got three francs and nine reali; see them?'

'If you don't get out of here I'll shoot you.'

'You? Like you shot your wife's friend! Like you shot your daughter's traitor!'

The old man, his face darker than his hood, his eyes green and red with anger and blood, took down his rifle and shot. Through the violet rifle smoke he saw the servant give a jump like the fawn and run away screaming.

Then he sat down in front of his cabin again, with the weapon on his knee, ready to defend himself if that one returned, with no regret for what he'd done. But the hours went by and no one appeared. Gloomy, quiet evening fell: the fog wrapped the horizon in a grey ribbon and the cows and heiffers lingered with their muzzles in the grass, as motionless as if asleep.

A rustling in the bushes startled the old man. But instead of his enemy he saw the fawn jump out and come up until it touched the rifle butt with its muzzle. He thought he was dreaming. He didn't move, and the fawn, not seeing the milk, put her head inside the cabin. Disappointed, she twirled around and went quickly back from where she had come. For a moment all was silent again.

The cat sleeping next to the fire woke up, got up, turned around and fell down again like a headband of black velvet.

Again the line of bushes quivered; again the fawn came out, jumped into the clearing. Immediately behind her jumped a buck (the old man recognized the male by his darker fur and by the branched horns), following her until he caught up with her. They leapt happily, one upon the other, falling together, resuming the race, the pursuit, the attack. The entire ancient landscape, pallid in the autumn evening, seemed to rejoice in their love.

A little later the gentleman farmer passed by with his plough coated with black dirt. This time he stopped.

'Baldassà, what have you done?' he said in a serious, but also slightly derisive, tone of voice. 'The judge is looking for you to arrest you.'

'Here I am!' answered the old man, serene once more.

'But why did you shoot your servant?' insisted the other, anxious to know the reason for the quarrel.

'Leave me alone.' Then the old man finally said, 'Oh, all right, you want to know why? It was over that little fawn whose eyes are just like my poor daughter Sarra's.'

The Ex-Schoolmaster

When it turned cold towards the end of November
the poorest men of the village – those who were not
even servants, who had no grain to sow, who didn't
even have a fire – would gather in the little entryway
of the shack where Maria Franchisca made dark
bread from a mixture of barley and wheat flour and
sold it at a very good price. After buying and eating
a loaf, they would lean against the wall or sit on the
floor, and linger there until evening. Not even then
would they all make a move to leave.

Some of the men brought something to eat with
the bread – a herring or a piece of goat cheese, white
and hard as marble – and also wine in a little black
gourd kept well hidden under their arm, and they
would drink and fall asleep.

The secret of that little cavelike entrance – without
a window, illuminated only by the light from the

48

oven in the adjoining kitchen and by the light from the door that opened and closed every once in a while – was its pleasant warmth and homelike sweetness.

When the door was wide open black mountains appeared in the distance, capped with ermine hoods of the first snow; and from there the wind came galloping down like a wild horse, throwing itself against the house and making everything shake; it chased the oven smoke back into the kitchen, intensifying little Maria Franchisca's glum mood and stubborn cough. Then she would go to the entryway, remonstrating against the customers who were loitering in words which were few but strong; the cough would cut her short, and some of the indigent customers would go away out of pity for her, to keep her from getting angry and coughing more; but two or three always stayed, deaf and silent, drawing into the corners like spiders, and not going away until evening.

The woman would end by leaving them in peace and going back to her work; then all that could be heard was the noise of the wind outside, continual and monotonous as the roar of the sea, and the tapping of the baker's paddle in the oven in the kitchen and the murmur of the flame.

From the entryway the men would watch the little mistress, slender and gentle as a child, and the gigantic woman baker, dark and scorched by the oven heat, coming and going, dragging chests, taking out the bread and cleaning off the ashes with a bunch

49

of mallow stems. A basket of hot bread beside the door spread the sweet odour of hay; the front door opened occasionally and women would come in, pushed by the sharp strength of the wind, their skirts puffed out, and would choose a loaf straight away and warm their hands and finally hold out a coin that Maria Franchisca dropped into her pocket without even looking at.

And so one day the schoolmaster came in with his hands in the pockets of his buttoned-up, worn-out jacket, a grey fringed scarf blown by the wind around his pale face fierce with hunger. He shut the door with his foot and went straight to the wicker basket to get a loaf of bread, without a bow, without looking at the men grouped in the entrance, without greeting the women. His thin, scornful face, whose slanting green eyes and protruding lower lip gave an air of savage mockery, was reddened for an instant by the reflection of the fire. He put the bread under his scarf and said on the way out, 'Maria Franchí, give me credit today; the town fathers will pay!'

The woman did not reply. She had stood up quickly as soon as she had seen him and had been standing there with her mouth and eyes open, white with fear. The men in the entrance didn't breathe either, as perturbed as though the strange event affected them personally. Because the master had been the employer and then the lover of Maria Franchisca. He had kept her in his house from the time she was a child; he had seduced her and then finally

50

chased her off with a stick, threatening her with death, because on her account he couldn't make a good marriage, he said. At school he had become cruel and arrogant with everyone who came near him. The town council had then fired him and he had brought a suit against it. He had been sentenced to pay the costs of the trial. Until a few months ago he could still be seen going around the village with his scornful air of superiority; he associated with no one; he looked at no one; but everyone still respected him because they feared him. Then he had disappeared and was believed to have found a place in some other village. Instead, here he reappeared with the return of winter and had gone to the house of his victim brazenly to steal her bread, just as he had stolen her honour and peace of mind. His footsteps weren't heard in the yard any more, but the woman and her customers inside hadn't yet recovered from their surprise. The baker, with the paddle in the oven, was letting the bread burn as she turned to look at her employer; and her employer was staring at the closed door with her big blue-green eyes in her childlike face, as though still unsure whether or not to believe the tragic apparition. However, with a leap she hurled herself into the entryway, slammed the door bolt shut, leaned her shoulder against the door as though to protect herself against an attack from outside, then, overcome, she gave a groan and fell in a faint.

The men picked her up; one carried her in his arms to her little bed in the small room behind the kitchen. She didn't revive. A thread of blood-tinged saliva drooled from her mouth.

'And she knew he would come back,' the baker said, bathing the woman's forehead with a rag dipped in wine. 'He had sent her word that she could finish paying the costs of the trial . . .'

'But, for God's sake, why not give her some warning?' said one of the men, offering his glass of wine for the dipping of the rag. 'If he comes back here I'll break his leg, God help me, I'll break his leg.'

'Why not give some warning?' repeated the other. 'We are human beings.'

But the baker motioned with her finger for them to go away. Maria Franchisca blinked her dazed eyes and with her little hand still white with dough wiped the wine from her cheeks.

'Come on, woman, cheer up; the bread is burning,' said the baker, helping her up; and they both went back to work.

From there in the entryway the men stood watching; nothing was said, but everyone understood that it was necessary to protect the poor lonely creature and to defend her from her tyrant's persecution. From time to time her tormenting cough was heard, and the howling wind outside seemed like the voice of her terrible enemy.

And yet when someone knocked on the door she ran to open it; it was a customer and she let her get some bread; she put the money in her pocket and did not replace the bolt. She seemed not to remember or fear anything any more, and later, since the men had not gone away, she began to grumble.

Then one of them, the one who had carried her in his arms, came resolutely forward. 'Maria Franchí, wouldn't it be better if one of us stayed here? Aren't you afraid?'

She looked at him in astonishment; she seemed to remember; she hesitated. 'No,' she finally said, 'I'll lock the door carefully.'

During the night it snowed. The customers were obliged to return because of the cold and curiosity, and because of a real feeling of disquieting pity.

The first to arrive was the man who had carried Maria Franchisca in his arms. He bought bread, questioned her with his eyes and seeing she was pale but calm he retired to his corner. Then the others arrived. Everyone was careful to stamp the snow from his shoes before entering, and this meant they did not intend to go away soon. Poor Maria Franchisca must not be left to the persecutions of her tyrant. But the hours passed and everything remained tranquil. The women worked. Outside lay the profound silence of days of snow, and it seemed like the cold had extinguished the world and its passions. And yet every time the door opened Maria Franchisca would turn with eyes open wide and seemed to be waiting in fear for someone to enter.

Towards evening she was taken by a great chill: her teeth chattered, she warmed herself at the oven in vain, and finally she burst into tears, wringing her hands.

'I'm afraid, I'm afraid,' she said.

The baker made her go to bed and gave her a drink of hot water with honey; with trembling hands she held the cup that clattered against her teeth and she kept repeating: 'I'm afraid . . .'

From out there the men were listening. And the one who had carried her in his arms came as far as the kitchen, saying to the baker in a low voice: 'Tell her to be calm. We will stay her to watch over her until that ass leaves town.'

Two of them, in fact, spent the night in the entrance. Maria Franchisca had a high fever and was delirious without ever mentioning her burdensome secret. She worried about burning the bread, the bad weather, the men who lingered by the door; but as for the rest, even in the face of death, she seemed to want to keep her pain and terror all to herself.

She stayed in bed for two weeks; the baker continued to bake the bread, helped by a neighbour woman, and the men didn't stop guarding her; the enemy outside was a little like the wind, there and not there, battering at the door but without coming in. The woman who helped make the bread made fun of Maria Franchisca's protectors.

'Who has seen him? No one in town has seen him. You're dreaming.'

And yet on Christmas Eve it was she, coming into Maria Franchisca's little room and helping her sit

up, putting a pillow behind her shoulders, who said,
'Now you are well; tomorrow you will get up; it's a
feast day. Listen to me, dove: the schoolmaster is at
my house, in our hay barn, lying on the ground
like a sick dog, and he doesn't eat, he doesn't want
anything; he only asks forgiveness for having frightened you. He has no house or food; to deny him
pardon is like denying it to the deposed Christ...'

The other was silent, looking at her with her large
eyes shining with tears.

'Maria Franchí. Today everyone forgives even their
worst enemy. Let him come and ask your pardon;
that way your fear will go away. What do you say,
dove? Yes?'

Yes, motioned the other with her head still damp
from feverish perspiration; and tears fell on her thin
neck and bounced on the sheet like pearls from a
broken necklace.

The kind woman stayed with her that night, and her
good friends in the entryway were sent away, since
Maria Franchisca was now well and didn't want company. The man who had carried her in his arms was
doubtful, however. He went to mass and, kneeling
down, shook his head as though chasing away some
bothersome thing in his hair. When he left the
church he followed a group of young men playing
an accordian. As he leaned against the wall listening
to the music he still seemed to be inside her house,
in the warmth, listening to the sick woman's moans
and feeling helplessly moved by her.

When everyone was at home, with the smoke and smell of roast pork floating over the courtyard gates, he went along the walls like a blind man until he reached her shack. There was a light. He knocked and the neighbour woman opened the door and let him in. She was kind to everyone.

He went as far as the kitchen and saw Maria Franchisca's enemy sitting next to her little bed. His legs were outstretched, his back resting comfortably against the chair, his hands in his pockets. She was sitting up on the little bed with her head bent to the right over the pillow supporting her, and in the palm of her hand was a pear he had brought.

However, the customer was not moved by the scene; an impulse of rage propelled him into the little room; he stammered, pointing to the convalescent, 'What are you doing, Maria Franchí, what are you doing?'

The ex-schoolmaster drew up his legs, and without rising, without taking his hands from his pockets, looked at him scornfully.

'Oh, oh,' he said, 'where do you think you are? Go away and don't put your nose in here again. Get out.'

And the kind woman led him by the arm to the door. He stayed outside, waiting for the master to go away. Dawn broke and only the kind woman came out of the little house. The tyrant remained inside.

Other customers arrived, protectors of Maria Franchisca, but after discovering from their companion that the master was there, they dared not enter.

To take revenge, they began to sing an insulting song – moving away, however, in a group; and the cold dawn wind beat against their backs and seemed to enjoy playing with their rags and scattering their voices.

The Thirteen Eggs

In a people that has an upper and lower class, there are, among the elevated classes, declining families who try to rise again by making good marriages for their children, and young men of the lower class who believe they can elevate themselves by marrying into such families, and young women who are sacrificed, and interested relatives who are always willing to fish in troubled waters.

The once rather well-to-do and respected Palas family, after many years of decline, hoped to improve their fortune by arranging a good marriage for their daughter Madalena. Sitting in the sun in their bare little dirt courtyard, Madalena and her stepmother sewed gaiters of rough wool for their men and often talked about the longed-for wedding. The stepmother, plump and perspiring, but with a still young, fresh face and large, sparkling black eyes, squirmed

58

on her cane stool, as her thimbled finger plied the flashing needle. Madalena, despite her nervous appearance, was immobile, her face as oval and white as an egg, shaded by a dark kerchief.

'We come from good stock, dear child,' said her stepmother, 'and time and fate can make and unmake everything – fortune and events – but cannot change one's origins. White bread is always white bread, even in a begger's sack, and spring water doesn't change even if pigs drink it. Yes, Golden Girl, they called your grandfather *Palas de ferru*, "Iron Back", so strong and powerful he was. Well, times have changed, and your brothers have gone to America along with other desperate men; but we are what we are, and if you marry Mauru Pinna, he will remain Mauru Pinna, son of a rich stonecutter, and you will remain the daughter of Franziscu Maria Palas.

Madalena did not reply, but raised her large, gentle eyes, sweet and golden as honey, and it seemed as though she were waking from a dream. With her white hands she adjusted the straps of her green velvet bodice, and the silk ribbon that adorned her rather long, blue-veined neck. Swift shadows, like those from low-flying swallows that almost graze one's head, darkened her golden irises from time to time.

'And besides, dear daughter, you are young and don't know something: people of good stock like us are clever and intelligent, while the lower classes are ignorant. You will be the mistress, Golden Girl, and Maureddu the servant. You will be able to give him

59

barley bread and dry ricotta when he goes to plough or harvest, and you will always be able to keep the coffee pot on the stove and make yourself fancy pastries and keep sweet cakes in your cupboard. He'll never notice, honestly.'

This reasoning convinced the girl, especially since the Palases – in this lovely season still far from harvest time – were nearly starving, in spite of the nobility of their stock. One day her stepmother had to borrow – at one thousand per cent – a half hectolitre of wheat; then she pawned her silver filigree locket, and after that she went to the valley to gather wild fennel and radishes.

Madalena never left the house. But spring came up to the little courtyard and covered the walls with buttercups and flowering moss; and on the roof of the little house the April wind shook the self-sown weeds and quivering sprigs of wheat that seemed to caress the blue sky above the worn roof tiles. Sometimes the pale seamstress grew hungry; then she would think about Maureddu Pinna and about his provisions of lard, wheat, cheese; and raising her violet-tinged eyelids she would watch the little white clouds of April with the vague gaze of starving convalescents.

Towards Pentecost Maureddu made his request. The go-between spoke at length with Madalena's stepmother.

'Maureddu Pinna? He can call himself a king in his own house. He has a good supply of everything;

he has oxen, a cart, a vineyard, a seed-bed. And he has no relatives to deplete his resources.'

'My stepdaughter, however, is a jewel,' replied the stepmother haughtily. 'She has gifted hands and is of good stock. If Maureddu Pinna were as rich as the sea he would never find her equal.'

At any rate he was accepted, and one evening went to make the first visit to his fiancée. Madalena was sitting next to the *focolare* sewing, while her father, an imposing man, with fine features and a reddish beard, was stretched out on a mat talking with his wife, embellishing his quiet conversation with proverbs and aphorisms.

'And so I tell you, my wife, the king in his carriage beats the hare. The wrongdoer often believes he's getting away with something because he's cunning. He runs just like the hare, but the king, the justice of the king I mean, in his slow but sure carriage, wins in the end.'

Suddenly Madalena felt something like an rubber ball bounce off her chest. She started, caught an orange in her lap, and raising her frightened eyes saw above the dark shape of the *antipetus* [a kind of masonry screen built between the door and the *focolare*], the dark, bearded face of her fiancé. It was he who had thrown the orange to announce his arrival; and he silently laughed at her fright, showing long pointed teeth between the black hairs of his moustache and beard.

'Welcome,' said the stepmother, rising. 'Aren't you coming in?'

Mauru came in: small and with his legs slightly bowed, in his new clothes with a hood on his shoulders, he looked like a medieval clown.

'Sit down,' his future father-in-law said without rising, but pushing a stool his way.

'I haven't come to stay,' the suitor replied.

Nevertheless he sat down and stayed there two hours, without ever looking at Madalena, who for her part never raised her eyes. She kept on sewing and the orange in her lap burned like a ball of fire. After talking about his fields, his oxen, his vineyard, and discussing with the stepmother and future father-in-law the financial worth of such and such a person, the fiancé went away.

The stepmother said, 'He's no beauty, but he's polite and kind-hearted.'

'Beautiful images are for hanging on the wall; men move and don't need to be handsome,' the father added, folding his long cap under his ear to make a pillow.

Madalena silently tossed the orange from hand to hand, then she got up, put it on the chair by the *antipetus* and went out into the small courtyard.

The new moon rose between the dark sprigs of wheat on the roof; from afar she heard a love song, vibrant and wild as the neighing of wild ponies in spring; from the kitchen came the smell from the orange that her stepmother was calmly eating, tossing the peel in the fire. Madalena dried her eyes on the sleeve of her blouse.

Every time her fiancé came he said he couldn't stay long, and he threw oranges, pears, and nuts to his fiancée from the *antipetus*. Once she put three tacks, sharp point up, on the stool where Maureddu usually sat, hoping that when he was pricked he would understand that she didn't like him and wouldn't come back again. He was pricked, but he said nothing, and he came back; but instead of sitting on the stool he leaned against the *antipetus*.

The wedding took place after the barley harvest. Although it was hot, the bride was pale and cold as a snow statue, and her new neighbours, seeing her so proud and reserved, began to speak badly of her. They called her, in fact, the 'Ice Saint'.

In the autumn Maureddu went to plough his land. His wife stayed alone in the house, and looking at her sacks of barley, beans, the overflowing chest of wheat, it all seemed like a dream.

Every morning her stepmother would come after mass and say, 'Try to fatten up so your husband will love you more. Don't you have eggs to make yourself some pastries?'

Madalena had all the staples, but she didn't have money to waste on extras. One day her stepmother noticed that the wheat chest had a hole in it and grain was spilling out.

'Do something, Golden Girl: sell the wheat and buy eggs and sugar. You can tell Maureddu that the ants have stolen the wheat from the chest a little at a time. He's simple-minded and will believe you.'

After the wheat it was the barley's turn.

'Tell your husband that the begging friars came by and the priors of Saint Francis and Saint Cosimo and that you gave them the barley for charity.'

Then they also depleted the oil and mixed water with the wine, and mice nibbled the cheese . . . But one day Madalena said, 'That's enough now. I'm fat enough.'

In fact she seemed like another person. Her face had taken on a dark, warm colour and her eyes sparkled like two stars in the dark evening sky.

With her blood enriched, an unusual energy ran in her veins; and when her husband returned, she was so adept at telling him lies that he looked at her with respect, and thought, 'She's become very nearly as wise and careful as her stepmother.'

Maureddu left again on Monday morning with the *bisaccia* of supplies over his shoulders. Some women of the neighbourhood who were going to the fountain caught up with him, and, looking at his *bisaccia*, they laughed and asked him: 'Has your wife given you some good things to eat, Maureddu Pí?'

'She's given me good things to eat; why, why do you ask?'

'It's just because she fasts when you're not there, and so you must be keeping Lent, too.'

'It's always Lent in a farmer's life,' he answered, going away with the slow pace of a man under a heavy weight.

A wild, disorderly swarm of clouds rose over Monte Albo and Monte Pizzinnu; and the whole sky over the valley from Orune to Nuoro became as dark as dusk. That moving, sad shadow even seemed to spread over the farmer's face.

He thought he was very clever and that everyone should respect him, particularly after he married Madalena. Instead, the neighbour women made fun of him just because of his wife. Why? What were they suggesting? Was she fasting? Perhaps they were hinting at the amorous deprivations of a wife when her husband was away? But if they were laughing it meant that Madalena didn't feel these deprivations too much.

Several days later he returned home unexpectedly and found a fire burning and Madalena roasting a nice piece of fat meat on the spit.

'We have a guest,' she said with some embarrassment. 'Your friend Juanne Zichina, who came from his town because of a quarrel he had with his brother . . .'

'Our guest is welcome. You've done right to treat him with honour.'

A little later Madalena's stepmother arrived, looking around and sniffing the air like a hunting dog; but her stepdaughter greeted her coldly and didn't even invite her to sit down.

Maureddu waited until midday; then, since the guest had not returned, he decided to leave again.

He had left his oxen grazing unguarded, and he was thinking that if some no-goods should see an ox without its owner they might be happy to substitute another for it.

Before he left the house he said to Madalena, 'How are you getting along with the neighbour women?'

'They aren't my kind,' she answered, twisting her mouth to one side; and he went away without daring to say any more.

But when alone he was again seized by his bad thoughts, because it is precisely in our solitude when the devil goads us like the farmer goads his drowsy oxen to make them move.

Maureddu began walking again. It was a beautiful December morning. Blue vaporous veils covered the distance; but as far as the eye could see the rocks and boulders appeared sharp and clear, as though polished; every blade of grass had a pearl dew drop, and the yellow leaves on the dark oak trees shone like gold coins.

Far away, on the valley path, Maureddu could make out a man on a horse, with a hood on his head and a rifle over his shoulder, and he recognized his friend Juanne Zichina who had come to Nuoro because of the customary quarrel. Maureddu didn't stop, and pretty soon Juanne Zichina caught up with him. They went the rest of the way together. The man on horseback began to talk about his quarrel, calling his brother the 'new Cain' because he had taken possession of a strip of land on a *tanca* that was common property; and the man on foot listened grimly, raising ironic and threatening eyes from time to time.

Juanne Zichina was a good-looking man of fifty – tall, ruddy, with a long black beard and shining teeth and eyes, sitting tall on his horse, with a cartridge pouch on his belt and spurs on his boots.

Next to him Maureddu felt small and awkward, and a strange thought, just like those the devil sends, crossed his mind.

On seeing the two men arrive together, Madalena frowned, but said nothing.

'Sit next to the fire, Juanne Zichí,' said Maureddu. 'My wife will give us something to eat and drink and you can go to the hearing like a satisfied fox . . .'

'Well, as I was telling you, dear brother, that new Cain also wanted to take the spring in the middle of the *tanca* . . .' the guest continued, sitting next to the *focolare*, after greeting Madalena. 'You'll tell me that the spring belonged to us both. No, now I'll explain . . .'

He took the steel hollow tube, taken from an old-fashioned rifle, that was used to blow on the fire, and began to trace some lines in the ashes piled in a corner of the *focolare*. Madalena was preparing the lunch basket. She drew near, obviously flustered, and began to stare at the guest in a strange manner, as though greatly struck by his story and by the sketch of the walls and paths of the *tanca* that he was drawing in the ashes.

'And so that Cain wanted to take this part for himself, that is, the woods and the asphodel pasture, and leave me the water meadow . . . I told him: brother, we are born to die, so let's try to come to a better understanding . . . Instead, he threw himself on me . . . we were right in front of that damned spring, which would be about here ... I yelled and the shepherds came running; otherwise Cain would have strangled me like the first one did his brother.'

'Oh, Jesus, Jesus!' shouted Madalena in turn, terrified, grabbing the barrel out of his hand.

Maureddu was also livid, and glared at his guest. But Zichina began to laugh, showing his strong teeth – white and straight as a wolf's. He got up and said, 'Now the judge will make everything right; I'm going to court.'

As soon as he left, Maureddu jumped up as though burned, and threw himself upon his wife like the new Cain had attacked his brother.

'Oh, you take up with strangers, with old boars? – wicked woman that I took almost dead from starvation!'

Madalena did not totter, she did not bend. She only put her hands on his chest to push him away, raising her face that had become the colour of yeast. Her eyes resembled live coals.

'That's the only reason I accepted you, because I was hungry; you, whose brain is as crooked as your legs! Let me go!'

A cruel smile illuminated her tragic face. She bent over the *focolare* and took two, five, thirteen eggs from the pile of ashes where Zichina had drawn the boundaries of the *tanca*.

'Here, look at them,' she said, bent over, with two eggs in the palm of her outstretched hand. 'Yes, I married you so I could eat, and I have taken wheat, barley, oil so I could buy pastries, coffee, eggs ... Do you see them? It was my stepmother who advised me to do it, and we have stolen and eaten together; but then I got tired and wanted to eat alone, and because she rummages through everything every time she comes here, I hid the eggs . . . I didn't want her to see them, or you either! . . . And much less the guest who would have laughed at us . . .'

The man listened in amazement. Then Madalena jumped up and began to throw the eggs at his head.

'Take them, you bastard . . . that's the way you threw oranges at me . . . take them . . . and I was boiling with rage and wanted to laugh when I saw you . . . take them; and go and complain to my step-mother if you aren't happy . . . Take them, you who dare to insult me as though I were your equal! . . .'

The eggs smashed against the head of the unfortunate man, and the runny yellow yolks coloured his face and chest with gold, while the whites slid to the floor. He howled like a calf, jumping head down here and there in the kitchen, wiping his eyes with his shirt sleeve, just like his wife had dried hers on the evening of their engagement.

The Counsellor's Christmas

The steamer was scheduled to leave at five o'clock, but by four-thirty it was full of third-class passengers – country folk with *bisacce*, soldiers on leave, prisoners who had served their sentences or were being transferred to the island's penal colonies, the *carabinieri* accompanying them. A little later the second-class passengers arrived, the petit bourgeois, salesmen, some students; and finally a small gentleman in a fur overcoat came on board, attended by porters weighed down by yellow leather luggage and cases and hat boxes. He was fat, with a pale beardless face, one hand in a grey glove, the other covered with massive gold rings.

An old dealer in oxen, who was travelling third class, with a *bisaccia*, recognized him and pointed him out to his companions, who then greeted him with deference, but also with a certain degree of respectful fear. The old dealer came closer to address him, but was pushed back by the porters and so waited for a more opportune moment.

In fact, once the traveller's luggage was put in a first-class cabin, he came out on deck and leaned against the railing to look at the landscape. Although it was the end of the year, the weather was nice and dry, the sea calm – grey towards the port, light blue on the horizon under the violet twilit sky.

In the clear cold air noises reverberated from the port and city still purplish from western reflections; just as on beautiful autumn evenings, a harmonica could be heard; a large red moon rose above the black mill tower and the surrounding water already reflected the splendour.

The traveller looked at the land and the sea, and his pale, flabby face and his cold, shallow blue eyes expressed neither admiration nor sadness; only his greyish lips showed an expression like disgust from time to time.

And now the old oxen dealer, who from his corner hasn't taken his bright black eyes from the important personage for an instant, believes the opportune moment has arrived for approaching him. When the boat leaves and the traveller goes back to his first-class cabin or to the deck reserved for first-class passengers, he won't have any way to pay his respects. Therefore the little old man bolsters up his courage and goes along the damp railing, rubbing his hand on his canvas trousers to wipe it clean before offering it to the traveller.

71

'Excuse me, Don Salvator Angelo Carta, if I may speak to you. I am . . .'

'Ziu Predu Camboni! How are you? Travelling?'

'I'm always travelling, Don Salvatorà! And how would I make it otherwise? We don't have a salary of two thousand scudi like your Lordship has. But it's true we don't have your talent either!'

'Where have you been?'

The little old man was returning from Rome and going back to his own town not far from Don Salvator Angelo's.

'It's been three years since I've seen you, Don Salvatorà! And why hasn't your Lordship come back to Sardinia for so many years? That's right: you have other things to think about. And now you're going to spend the holidays with your family? How happy your nephews will be. They talk of nothing but you.'

'My nephews? They are all good for nothings and are waiting for me to die!' Don Salvator Angelo said roughly, and instead of protesting the little old man began to laugh.

'Remember, Don Salvatorà, when I came to your town to buy calves from your grandmother? You were a student then, a happy soul, with special little caps with ribbons like women wear. "That one there," Donna Mariantonia, your grandmother, may she be with God in heaven, would say, "that one is a little sparrow that will peck all the sour figs." And she complained to me, may she be with God in heaven, because your Lordship wouldn't leave the neighbour women or maidservants in peace. You jumped over

72

walls like devil. Remember that pretty little maid, tall
and brown, that seemed like a palm tree? Her name
was Grassiarosa, and your Lordship ran after her
like you were bewitched. But Donna Mariantonia was
mistaken, even if she was as wise as an abbess, may
she be with God in heaven. Yes, her other grand-
children have eaten sour figs and you . . . you have
become the pride of the town!'

'Eh, imagine that!'

A respectful wonder elongated the woody, burnt
face of the old nomad.

'That seems little to you? Counsellor of the Court
of Appeal?'

'There are higher places.'

'If there are, you will reach them. If there was still
the viceroy they would make you that . . .'

Don Salvator Angelo smiled, flattered in spite of
himself, and asked for news of the town and acquaintances. Times were bad, the crops hadn't been good;
everyone had some kind of trouble, and people were
going to America and other countries, like the Jews
in Moses's time. Many had died and many other
disappeared and nothing was known of them, as
though swallowed by the sea. Among the dead was an
old servant of Don Salvator Angelo's grandmother, a
certain Bambineddu, called that because he was
a simple man. Bambineddu had married the pretty
Grassiarosa, the 'palm tree' who had once pleased
her noble little master.

'And what became of her?'

'Her? She is a widow with six or seven children all

skinny as a finger. Not long ago I saw her at a railway crossing house with a flag in her hand. Yes, the crossing house before you get to Bonifai Station, where I think her brother is crossing-keeper – he too is a widower with a parcel of children. She had a hungry look.'

The clanging of chains and shriek of sirens filled the air with dreadful noise; the steamer pulled out, puffing like a sea monster that had suddenly woken up and was in a hurry to return to the high seas.

Soon land was far away, wrapped in evening haze, but the moon followed the ocean travellers and lit their way on the infinite desert of the sea. A deathly pallor made Don Salvator Angelo look even sadder: disturbed by going away from the mainland, or remembering the young 'palm tree' and remorseful for having loved and forgotten her?

Ziu Predu Camboni looked at him almost maliciously; but when Don Salvator Angelo, staggering, turned to leave and said through clamped teeth, 'I always get sick, even when the sea is calm . . .' the little old man went with him as far as the golden entrance to first-class and realized that the mysterious malady the Counsellor was fighting was the most terrible that man sometimes gets: sea sickness.

'Why go if it makes you suffer?' Ziu Predu Camboni asked himself and returned to his third-class quarters, where soldiers were singing and convicts were dozing, bound like slaves.

'Why go if it makes you suffer?' Don Salvator Angelo

asks himself, stretched out motionless on his white bunk. And he feels a deep anguish and seems to be on the back of a wild beast that is running across an immense and dangerous desert. If you move you are lost: lie as still as possible and think of the day when you won't move any more!

He feels terror, as though death were near: the saddest and happiest memories, the most hated and dearest ghosts crowd around him. The cabin seems like a tomb where he has laid every vanity and every ambition.

'Why go if it makes you suffer?' Don Salvator Angelo asks himself, while the wind blowing in the clear night beats against the little window like a night bird whistling, groaning, wanting to come and rest. 'It's always like this: to go is to suffer. To suffer for others, for the childish grandmother, for useless relatives, for undisciplined nephews, for wild brats: always the same, to *keep going* for the others. Ah, viceroy? . . . Yes, since a boy, before wearing the little hat with the ribbons, before jumping over walls (ah, Grassiarosa the 'palm tree', how sweet and supple you were!), I dreamed of becoming viceroy, or even king, for the pleasure of being able to go around, to go disguised, into the huts of the poor and leave them money and pearls . . . I was a fine example of a romantic boy. Even then I was thinking of others . . . When have I ever thought of myself? In good times or bad always thinking of others; and yet I pass for a fine example of selfishness and my dear nephews say I don't take a wife because I'm sure she would run away . . .'

His nephews? Six of them also, like Grassiarosa's brats. Grassiarosa is in a little house just before the station of Bonifai. He will be there just as she appears with her flag . . .

The thought of arrival fills him with a boy's joy. To arrive, to get out of that bed of agony, to live again! He seems to see the wild, picturesque gulf, with the mountains, islands, rocks covered by night's veil, but as though illuminated by a distant reflection; he seems to smell the island, the scent of the scrubland, and his joy is such that he believes he's returned to his youth, to have his senses still burning from the memory of Grassiarosa, tall and supple as a palm tree . . .

The train runs across rocks and scrubland; here is the deep sky of the island, the horizons of a distant youth . . . here is the desolate plain of Bonifai, with the little grey hill in the background and the black village on the grey hill, with the wandering flocks, rocks, swampy streams. Here is a dry wall, grey and greenish like a large snake sleeping in the pale dawn of winter; distant mountains are covered in a lavender fog. A lamp shines in the little house before the station. A worn out, emaciated woman stands motionless beside the crossing gate with a flag in her hand, and a crowd of ravenous, dirty children swarm around her. And all the anguish of sea sickness again seizes the body and soul of Don Salvator Angelo Carta.

After the train passed, the woman with the flag went back into the little house and lit a fire in the large fireplace, the only luxury in the damp, wretched room that served as shelter for the crossing keeper and his double family. And soon, like moths attracted by light, the little children and bigger ones, who up to that moment had fearlessly challenged the cold in the yard and scrub around the little house, gathered around the widow still bent over the fireplace.

How many were there? As many as chicks around a hen: two, the smallest, seized the woman's hips; the two biggest, who ran around laughing, threw themselves on her back; another, in order to escape persecution from a little girl in a red cap whose large black eyes gleamed savagely out of a dark little face, got between the fireplace and the widow's legs; and all together they formed a group that by the colour of their faces and clothes seemed made of bronze.

Shadows of the dishevelled heads danced on the walls and ceiling in the red light of the flame; and the woman, half tenderly, half savagely, tried to free herself from the entanglement, pushing first one and then the other, speaking harshly and sweetly.

'Now that's enough; get up from there Bellia, or I'll spank you; Grassiedda, dear heart, don't tear my blouse; it's torn enough; and you, Antonie, you devil, stop it; I'll tell your father when he comes home; I'm tired of your misbehaving. You're old enough to help me and instead you bother me. I've had enough of all of you!'

Antonietta, the one in the red cap, swore under

her breath, then went to sit in the corner by the door, as though in ambush; and the woman continued her scolding, attaching the pot to the hook over the fireplace, something that finally convinced the children to be quiet. Some of them sat in a semicircle around the fireplace, others helped the woman take from a basket the long dark macaroni she had made that morning. It was Christmas Eve; and even for the poorest of the poor, even in the most desolate loneliness, this is a good time to forget their misery. Boil, little pot, fry, little pan, with the sauce made with oil and flour! . . . Even the poor have their day, says a Sardinian proverb. Anyway, in spite of her complaints, Grassiarosa was not sad; she never had been; why would she want to start now? Like those children gathered around her without giving her too much to do, crying and laughing about every little thing, she didn't worry about her fate or think about the future, and if she thought about the past it was to draw comfort from it.

'On nights like this! How my employers used to celebrate! Whole suckling pigs were roasted; and they sang all night. What happiness, *Santa Maria bella*! But even they, now, have finished feasting, and leave the pigs to whomever has them. Only one of my employers is still rich; I think he is richer than Ziu Predu Camboni, the dealer who comes to buy oxen. He had seemed the happiest, that little master, and he became the most serious; but who knows if even he is happy! I think I saw him on the train this evening. His face was as pale and swollen as a fresh cheese . . .'

The children burst out laughing; but she was serious, talking more to herself than to them.

'What's so funny? Can't the rich be pale?'

'The stationmaster is red as an apple,' Bellia said, in a tone that did not invite argument.

Shortly the macaroni was cooked and seasoned. Grouped around the woman, the children were looking at the bowl like an invaluable treasure; the only thing disturbing their greedy joy was the thought of having to wait for their father and uncle.

'At least give us the saucepan,' begged Antoneddu, a ruddy little fellow with big green eyes.

'You'll see, I'll lick it so clean you won't have to wash it.'

'I'm keeping some for Battista in the pan. If he's late coming home – and if he's gone to the village and the tavern, he'll certainly be late – we'll go ahead and eat.'

Then the children looked out of the door, pushing each other as far as the low wall to see if the crossing keeper was coming. The moon rose over the mountains of Nuoro, yellow as a flame; it climbed from one long black cloud staining the pale evening sky to another. The railway tracks shone alongside the road like threads of water, and in the dim light the bushes and rocks resembled sleeping animals.

The children were superstitious, but also courageous; they kept waiting to see legendary horses and dogs come running past, or the devil dressed like a shepherd, with a herd of damned souls changed into boar, or to see a woman in white sitting on a high hill spinning the moon. Antoneddu lived in anticipation of seeing the Madonna walk by dressed like a little beggar woman; Grassiedda, the little fair-haired stutterer, watched to see the sky open up and reveal the flaming world of truth through luminous doors. And Antonietta thought with terror, but also with a certain pleasure, of Lusbé, the chief of devils; and Bellia, the braggart of the group, claimed to have already seen a giant, a comet, the Antichrist himself sitting on a black donkey.

It was he, therefore, who went as far as the gate of the barred road that evening and came back saying that coming along the tracks was a black man with a mane on this neck and a yellow box in his hand . . .

'Could he be the devil dressed like a gentleman?'

His siblings and cousins began to tease him, but they grew silent and pale, and some ran into the little house when the mysterious figure appeared at the gate and walked across the yard.

'Zia, Zia, mamma, mamma, a black black black man . . .'

The woman ran to the door and in the light of the lamp recognized the man she had seen on the train; pale, fat Don Salvator Angelo. What had he come for? Childishly she thought: 'He has heard that I am a widow and he is coming to see me . . . like before!' And then remembrance that she was nearly old now, wan and worn out, made her laugh.

'Look how I am!' she murmured, crossing her

80

arms over her chest in order to hide her torn bodice. But he put a finger to his lips, and she in turn, noticing that Antonietta was approaching, made no other sign that she recognized the mysterious gentleman.

He went straight to the fireplace, sat down, put the yellow box next to him.

'All right then, what's the news? Tell me.'

She began to talk, sometimes crying, sometimes laughing, with that carefree, happy laugh that still flowered on her face like roses blooming on ruins. But the man was paying more attention to the curious, anxious children who had again gathered around her than to what she was saying. Observing those beautiful, wild heads, those black dusty curls, that red hair and yellow plaits golden in the reflection of the flame, those black eyes and those green eyes that watched him in fascination, charming him with joy and sadness at the same time, he thought: 'If I had married her all these little rascals would be mine.' And he imagined a beautiful dining room suitably bourgeois, with a Christmas tree on the table, and these children all dressed in lace and velvet, and that beautiful little blonde with big cat's eyes rocking upright in a chair, reciting a poem for the occasion.

No. It was better this way. It was more picturesque, more romantic, and even more comfortable. And suddenly the man in black took off a glove and stretched a finger towards a dark little dimpled face where a great mischievious joy seemed to shine.

'You, little scoundrel, what is your name?'

81

'Murru Giovanni Maria, or also Bellia.'

'Do you go to school?'

'Yes, sir.'

'At Bonifai?'

'Yes, sir.'

'Even when it rains or snows?'

'That doesn't bother me!' Bellia said haughtily. Pushed by the woman, he stood before the stranger, while his brothers and sisters and cousins looked at him and at each other, struggling to hold back their laughter: the laughter of envy, of course. But then the man in black turned to the whole group.

'Have you eaten?'

For a reply some began yawning.

'Perhaps you would like to eat something while waiting for Battista? Murru Giovanni Maria, help me open this box. Slow down, careful! It's what's at the Bonifai station; it's not the London station. Oh, better put it here on the table.'

'What are you doing? What a bother for you! You'll get dirty!' shouted the woman, running around in her confusion.

'Calm down! There, it's done . . .'

Like flies around the honey jar, the heads of the children crowned the edge of the table. And on it, as happens in fables at the touch of a magic wand, appeared so many good things. Even pears, yes, even grapes – in those times! – even a yellow bottle with a golden neck!

'I like red wine,' Bellia declared, and the woman

82

shouted at him, 'Smart aleck, smart aleck!' But the man in black said, 'You are right!'

Slowly and solemnly the distribution began, and so there would be no injustice, the group was made to line up in order of age; but when everyone had his portion and permission to disperse, there was general flight and many went outside to be able to talk freely.

Only Antonietta maintained her quiet, observant calm. Leaning against the doorway, with one foot over the other, her red cap in the shadows, she watched the stranger and thought of Lusbé. Yes, Jesus Christ and Saint Francis dressed like poor men to go around in the world; only Lusbé wore rich clothes and put on rings and chains of gold . . .

But the calm voice and the local accent of the mysterious gentleman brought her back to reality.

'We can have a bite, too, Grassiarò! Last night I didn't close my eyes. Today I slept on the train and didn't eat . . . Sit down there. Here, take a little of this pie . . . Tell me about the business of the shop you were speaking of a little while ago! . . .'

She hesitated, shy and flustered, but ended by taking the pie and beginning to talk. Yes, before leaving for America her husband had opened a general grocery. Things had gone well, but the capital was not his, and he had gone away with the hope of earning it himself. Instead the wind of death had blown him and his little fortune away. She wiped her eyes with fingers greasy from the pie.

'Come on, Grassiarò! There are still good people

in the world. You might find the small capital to get your store going again. But are you clever at selling? If you are clever at selling and buying again, the rest takes care of itself.'

She looked at him with eyes open wide; then she burst into tears, but stopped immediately and made the sign of the cross. Just at the moment from the village on the hill came the sonorous ringing of bells – distant, sweet, like the tinkling of grazing flocks. The bells rang for mass.

'He'll run away if he's Lusbé!' Antonietta thought, seeing her aunt making the sign of the cross; and she made it also and all the others imitated her.

But instead of running away, the man in black took the bottle and began to scrape away the golden paper with his finger.

'Grassiarò, come on! You know the Sardinian proverb: "Even the poor have their day." Now, then, what will we put in this shop? Help me uncork this bottle and bring some glasses.'

She had only one glass, but it was a large one. First the beautiful golden wine of Solarussa was given to the children to taste.

'Take it easy, oh! It's *vernaccia*, you know; it will make you crazy. Ah, you, Bellia! You said you like only red wine! I think you'll like this white, too. And now it's our turn.'

The woman washed and dried the glass and put it in front of the black gentleman; his hand was trembling, but his wrinkled mouth smiled again.

'You again!' she said under her breath, and added out loud, 'But why all this?'

Why? He didn't know why himself. He only remembered that his nephews said he had a liking for everything, and he answered, 'Just because it makes me happy. Drink!'

She refused the beautiful golden wine once, twice; but was finally forced to take it. And they both drank from the same glass like once long ago.

What the hell was this story about?

I can't make head or tail of it!

The Marten

One Thursday in April little Minnai woke up thinking, 'Today I want to have some fun,' and he jumped up naked from the foot of the little bed where he slept with his young aunt. Nude, thin, dark, with his ribs trembling, his long reddish hair tousled around his little oval face, he resembled little Saint John in the picture over the little bed. Except that the eyes of the painting were soft and brown, and his blueish-green eyes flashed with mischief.

For a time he ran naked here and there around the small, low little room lighted by a skylight with two glass panes. His clothes, shoes, shirt were on the black chest. But he wanted to enjoy himself, that is, to do something different from other days, so he began by proposing to go barefoot and not wear his shirt or vest or underpants. Besides he had never understood what good those things were, just as he

86

did not understand why his grandfather made him go to school when all his being yearned for the vineyard – the vineyard where his uncle had gone to weed that day after shutting him up alone in the house with his book bag. Even more than the vineyard, he yearned to go to the pasture next to it, with the sheep, the black dog, grandfather's red horse, his *bisaccia*, grass, stones to throw at passers-by from behind the low wall, and above all to be with the boar, deer, eagles and martens.

'But today . . . today . . .'

His mind was made up: he would escape, break through the skylight, run along the roof, fly.

Sitting on the chest he put on his shorts, making terrible faces and sticking his tongue out at the books and the ink waiting there on the table under the skylight. The worst curses he had ever heard drunk men say on holiday evenings welled up in his throat, but he did not repeat them aloud because it was a mortal sin. He hated his book bag and wanted to have a good time that Thursday, but he didn't want to go to hell.

A jump, a shake, and his shorts were up. He didn't need braces or buttons; a string would do, a nice strong string that's always good to have. Besides holding up shorts, a piece of string could come in handy when you were going to have some fun. If, for example, you have to make a snare for a marten, or a weasel, there's nothing better. A piece of string is always good for something; and so is a match, a scrap of paper, buttons, nails, that spool of thread stolen from his aunt's sewing basket. All these things Minnai pulled from the stuffed pockets of his shorts, examined carefully and put back again.

There, done. And his jacket? Where's his jacket? He looks everywhere. The jacket is not to be found, not inside the chest or out, not under the bed or in the kitchen. His aunt has hidden it. Everything is shut up and dark. It seems like a house of death with the fire out, the door locked, the cold white milk in the chipped bowl there on the oven next to the bread.

Minnai went to the door and shook it; it wouldn't open. He looked through the crack but saw only a corner of their lonely garden with the wall separating it from the garden of the house nun, Donna Antonina. Minnai was also cloistered, like the mysterious neighbour whom no one knew because she had made herself a prisoner for twenty years. But he didn't want to be a monk, no, no, not even a priest like his grandfather wanted. He'd rather die. He squatted down in front of the door, following the line of light from the white crack like a candle, and he began to cry, toying with the ends of his string. Yes, he knew what it was to be orphaned, without any land of his own, made to go to school to become a priest or farm manager; forced to give up everything, even going barefoot, even going naked. 'Nothing! I want to do nothing nothing nothing!'

He jumped up again. He had to put on his shirt and his vest and school smock also. It was almost cold inside, even though the swallows' cries outside quivered in the silence as on summer evenings. The bowl of cold milk only increased the sadness of his little heart. He should sit down at the table under the skylight; but that smooth black leather bag before him, with its chewed straps, was the coldest and most horrible thing in the house. It was repulsive to touch, it was something putrid, it was the black shroud of a small dead monster. Better to look up, up towards the skylight. Up there is air, sky, life – life!

There is also the cat's white face that seems to invite Minnai to have courage, to try to break out of his shroud. Yes, sometimes the example of a being infinitely weaker than we are is enough to call us back from the dark depths of our misery. Besides, it wasn't the first time Minnai had taken a lesson from the cat. In a flash, then, a large cork container that his aunt used for storing flour was on the table, upside down like a huge drum, with the black bag buried under it; and on that a chair, and on the chair a stool, and on to the stool, as if climbing a tower, went little Minnai, who broke through the skylight so that his head emerged into the infinite. The cat had run away in surprise. Everywhere on the low, age-old roofs (the roof tiles had become again a crust of fertile earth) flourished wild grasses, hay, oats, weeds, giving Minnai the illusion of open spaces which rewarded him for his courage.

But as soon as he was up he noticed two bad things: his hand was bleeding, and a wall on the right with a little window flush to the roof stood between him and the horizon. Minnai wasn't very worried about the blood; he would have given it all for a soldo, if it would have bought a nest with three little birds inside. And besides he could suck and swallow the blood and get it back inside and nothing is lost. The important thing was to climb over the little window and get up on the higher roof.

So, very carefully, he takes a step. He is afraid of falling through the roof, he feels so big and heavy; thieves in the night must walk like this when they do what they like doing. A nice thing being a thief; living on roofs, going in houses where people are sleeping, taking other people's things as though they were yours: perhaps there was nothing nicer in the world. Maybe it's even nicer to live on roofs than in the vineyard or sheepfold. Except that there is no way to hunt. And yet, yes; look. A screech across space. Minnai throws himself on all fours on the tiles and lets the hawk come closer. Look, it's almost above his head, black, wings spread, so near he sees its eyes shine, gilded by the sun. Yes, yes, one could even hunt on the rooftops. Minnai leaps up and launches his aunt's spool in the direction of the hawk, holding the end of the thread between his bloody fingers. But the hawk doesn't fall and the spool disappears. The hawk is way up in the sky, the spool is beyond the roof, in Donna Antonina's garden. Minnai winds up the thread into a jumble which, even tangled like that, can still be useful.

He went over to the little window which immediately opened up under his eyes like a white well. It was a narrow, high room, with bare whitewashed walls. There was a step ladder for opening and closing the little window. Down below, in the clear half-light, next to a little bed covered with a coarse material, a little nun dressed in black sat on a stool. She had a rosary in her hand and in her lap an animal that looked like a yellow cat.

As soon as Minnai stuck his head inside, the nun raised her startled face and the animal slipped from her lap. Long, with a tail longer than its body, it seemed to disappear underground. She bent down to call it from under the little bed, but as it did not come out, she again raised her frightened little face.

'Go away,' she implored in a whisper.

But from up there Minnai asked calmly, 'What kind of animal is it? It's not a cat, it's not a dog.'

'It's a marten. But go away! See how you frightened it? Go away.'

Minnai was unaccustomed to obeying. And besides he intended to enjoy himself that day.

'I know who you are,' he said from above. 'You are Donna Antonina, the house nun. You've been here a hundred years and my aunt has never met you. But my grandfather has. He says that you were beautiful and that you shut yourself up in the house because your husband left you.'

The woman gasped. Her eyes became veiled with tears. The little boy's voice seemed like a voice from her past. Ah, then, she was remembered in the world? And where was the world? She was suddenly overwhelmed by jumbled recollections of the past.

'Who is your grandfather?'

'You don't remember? Salvatore Bellu. My grandfather is rich. We have a vineyard, pasture land, a hundred sheep and a horse and other things. I go to school. But why doesn't that animal come out? Oh, I forgot: we also have beehives. If you want me to I can make the marten come out from under the bed. I know about these things. One time I caught three martens, and another time nine. It's wonderful the way they stand still when they see me. I also catch goshawks with a thread.'

The woman listened and believed what she heard: all her life she had always believed everything.

'Come down,' she said to the little boy.

In a flash he was down; he reached under the bed, took the panting animal and put it back in the woman's lap. The marten looked at him, its clear eyes full of fear, while it licked the hand of its mistress.

'How long it is! While pulling it out it seemed to grow longer, like dough. And that golden neck, the little teeth, those whiskers, and that tail like a new little broom!' he said, caressing it. 'How did it get here? It must be the one I caught once that got away. We live near here.'

'When did it run away from you?'

'Eh, it would be about three years now.'

'But how old are you?'

'Who knows? I'm an orphan. Maybe eight.'

'And at five you were already hunting martens?'

'Yes, even when I was three. You can go hunting whenever you like.'

'But I've had this animal for barely a year.'

'Yes, a year ago I also caught a lot of them. My grandfather takes them to a man who gives him a new rifle for each one.'

Meanwhile he had sat down cross-legged at the feet of the nun and was languidly watching the marten. The desire to take it away with him was making him drunk.

'My nice, nice, little animal,' he said, leaning his head on his right shoulder and smiling at it. The marten, as though fascinated by the boy's passion, began to lick his bloody little hand.

He stayed there like that all morning. The nun asked him for news of the world of thirty years ago, and he answered without hesitation; for many things, and men and what they do – everything, in fact – never change. Towards noon someone knocked on the door.

'It's my niece who brings me food. Hide, even though she never comes in here,' said the nun. He hugged the marten to his chest and hid under the little bed.

And while he felt it palpitate against his own heart he murmured with the pangs of a lover: 'Mine! Mine! All mine! I'll take you away with me no matter what. I've finally caught you! Yes, I've got you and you're mine. But I won't take you to the man in exchange for a rifle. No, I'll keep you with me, I'll hide you in the wood pile, I'll come to sleep with you, and I'll bring you my aunt's chicks, and even her cakes, if you want them, because I know where to find them and how to open and close the cupboard secretly.

I'll bring you everything; and so we'll have fun together, and be happy together. What are you doing in this prison? Are you a nun too? No. I ran away from prison, you know. I broke out of the roof. And one day we'll go away together, to the country, behind the vineyard wall. There we'll be comfortable; yes, there where there are no people, no school. My dear heart . . .'

The marten licked his ear.

In the mean time the nun had wordlessly brought back the basket of provisions, and she began to prepare the table.

'Come out,' she called quietly.

But those two beneath the bed seemed to be dead; dead, embracing, buried in their dream of love and liberty.

'Let us stay here,' Minnai said finally. 'It's nice here. Just give us something to eat. I'm used to staying under the bed, when my aunt wants to beat me. Then I eat and read and even write under the bed. I sleep there, too.'

But the nun wanted her companion. She wouldn't know how to live without it. Even the marten grew restless at the smell of food and grew longer like a snake, warm and soft on Minnai's chest, pushing its clawed paws on his neck, hiding his slender snout under his arm. Finally it managed to slip away from his arm and Minnai followed it out.

There was plenty of food, and wine, too; after clearing the table the nun went back to her place, with the marten stretched out on her knees with its head hanging down on the right and its long tail on the left. She began telling him things about her own world even though Minnai, half-asleep, hadn't asked her.

'You should know that once someone said: you are as if dead to me. Well, then, what could I do? Truly become like a dead woman. In the beginning, I remember, I cried so much that my eyes got used to crying; the tears came without my noticing. Like a fountain spouts water. But then I thought: to die today or thirty years from now is the same thing. Yet, thinking it over, you say a lot of things, but when you're alive you're alive; prisoners who've committed a crime are comforted by thinking of that far-off day of freedom, thinking about the day they'll see the sun on the road. But someone who has made himself a prisoner without guilt, by his own will? You have a lot of time to think about death, and the company of the living is still pleasing. So for many years I had the desire for company, then I didn't think about it any more. Finally, a year ago, this marten jumped down from the little window, like you did, and hid under the bed. At first I thought it was a cat; but I looked closer and was frightened; it looked at me in fear, too, and began to run, but it didn't see the ladder to escape. Then I felt very sorry for it and thought: if I let it go they'll kill it. I closed the window and stood still; so the marten quietened down and hid under the bed again. I put out a little bread and water and didn't close my eyes all night. I was afraid it would jump on me, so I left a candle burning. But late at night I heard it move and stretching my neck I saw that it was drinking. It was panting while it drank, stopping to listen, frightened. I began to cry and would have liked to put it in bed to comfort it. And so as the days went by the animal got used to drinking and eating and was no longer afraid. One day I picked it up: it didn't struggle; it was as soft as grass in the springtime. It had swollen paws; that's why it didn't run away; I put tallow on them, but it cured itself by licking them, and even after it was healed it didn't try to run away. And here it is. It is good and keeps me company; I feel like I'm still in the world when I'm with it. It's like a daughter; my love,' she concluded, stroking it with her trembling little hand.

The marten had closed its eyes and lay as still as death.

Minnai was listening, but nothing about the nun's story mattered to him. His longing to have the marten and take it away overwhelmed him so strongly that he wanted to cry. Tears fell without his noticing. 'Like water falls from a fountain.'

'Let me hold it a little bit more; then I'll go . . .'

Touched, the nun took the sleeping marten from her knees and he in turn began to caress it, plunging his little hand with delight in the fur as soft as tender March grass.

Down from the little window the afternoon sky sent a blue reflection, a distant light, as from the mouth of a well. Up there was joy, liberty; there was the solitude of the vineyard and the scrub, life, life!

Minnai was silent, waiting, having decided to wait even a thousand years and a thousand days to achieve his purpose. Every once in a while he raised his bright eyes and saw the eyes of the nun veil over, close, open, and close again.

When Minnai was sure the house nun was in a deep sleep he got on his knees as though asking her pardon. He made the marten comfortable on his neck like a sleeping baby and climbed silently up the ladder, taking care not to crush its tail.

The Open Door

On holy Wednesday Simone Barca went to confession. He was desperate, and a desperate man's thoughts turn to God, just as a sick man's turn to a doctor.

Simone went to the basilica, a national monument that still enhances the declining town; at that hour in the morning only some friars from the adjoining monastery were celebrating mass in the chapels where dampness had covered ancient frescoes with a layer green. The women of the Barbagia region, with hoods on their heads and coarse narrow skirts fastened with little silver chains, chanted the rosary in their local dialect. Their voices were lost in the vastness of the basilica as in the ruins of a temple, and the wild odour of euphorbia and blooming alder came from the valley through the wide open doors. Simone went to confess to the prior, whose huge body filled the little confessional, and who was breathing heavily and snorting inside there like a bear in a cage.

'Father, I'm a lost man. I'd like to kill someone I'm so desperate. I have committed the worst of sins. Until a short time ago I was the son in a family, Father, the only son. I was still sleeping with my mother when I was twenty years old; but right after she died, bad companions settled on me like flies on a raisin seed; and my uncle, who is also a priest, instead of helping me, chased me out of his house and turns away when he sees me. Yes, I've committed all the worst sins. I've played cards, drunk, gone with bad women, consulted a fortune teller. I've sworn in vain, I've wished my neighbours misfortune, I've coveted the goods of others, I've forged . . . yes, Father . . . I forged a signature, and in a few days the promissory note is due . . . and I'll have go to go prison and I'll be dishonoured . . . All the fault of bad companions who have now abandoned me. All doors are now closed to me . . . there is not even one door open to me! I'm sorry, Father; I'll go to prison and pay for the crime, but give me the Lord's absolution so I can make a good Easter and suffer in innocence like Christ Our Lord.'

The prior breathed heavily and didn't answer. Simone, with his thin, black Bedouin's face in his hands, also breathed hard and thought: 'Maybe he's scandalized. Or maybe it made him happy to hear that the cause of my ruin is basically my uncle, Father Barca. Brothers and priests don't see eye to eye.

Perhaps, to spite my uncle, he'll give me money to pay the note.'

But the prior snored and said nothing. His hot breath touched Simone's face. Tired of waiting, the penitent shook himself from his dream of expiation and gloomy thoughts; he peered in with his large, dark, child's eyes and a bitter smile over his dimpled, clean-shaven cheeks. The priest was asleep. Ah, even the Lord is deaf to the cries of the desperate sinner.

Simone went away quietly, with his heart full of sadness and his mind agitated by ugly thoughts. Around the main altar services were beginning, and already the happy voice of Father Barca could be heard warbling the psalms. People came and went. Even men came at this time – tall, with long, square beards like in Moses' time, dressed in leather jackets and short, wide twill trousers, similar to short skirts. Some seemed like prophets, so solemn, calm and simple were they; others were small, thin, like our Simone, burned by the wind and bad thoughts. Even the women resembled biblical characters. One of them that Simone encountered in the basilica courtyard, a widow, tall and dry, with an olive complexion and large greenish eyes, enclosed in her hieratic clothes like a black sheath, needed only corn sheaves in her hand to make her look like a second mother-in-law of Boaz. Simone was startled by the sight of her, he was startled by hate, since this woman was a kind of housekeeper for Father Barca, and also startled by the sudden thought that there was no one in his uncle's house just at this moment; and as though it had all at once become night, he began to see things and people indistinctly and he walked warily along by the walls, stumbling on the rocks encumbering the rough roads. In this state he reached his house that resembled a ruined tower, and only then did it seem that light came back to his surroundings.

Simone went inside and a little later his face appeared at the window on the second floor of the two-storey house, a face as thoughtful as a general's pondering a battle plan from a high fortress. Simone's battlefield was the brief panorama spread before his eyes, composed of a path intersected by a ditch where reeds and grass took root as though in open countryside, the widow's small house opposite his and the large dark house and courtyard of his priest uncle's between the widow's house and a small chapel, whose little garden – invaded by weeds and shaded by cypresses – looked like the corner of a cemetery. Simone remembered that he had spent his childhood and adolescence jumping the wall between his uncle's courtyard and the church garden. He asked himself if this wasn't his chance to go through the exercise once again, but in reverse, that is, from the church garden to his uncle's court-yard. Once there it was easy to get inside the fortress, that is, into his uncle's house. No one knew better than he the openings, hallways, mazes. Closing his eyes he could see the wall projection on the landing where Father Barca put the big key to his room before leaving the house; opening his eyes again he

recalled with some excitement that large and somewhat mysterious room, illuminated by a little lamp,
full of sacred images and bound books, where more
than once as a boy he had surprised his uncle in
shirt sleeves and skullcap counting his gold coins like
a sorcerer, or perforating his name on banknotes
with a pin. One day, walking on all fours on the floor
and scratching around, the better to imitate a wild
boar, Simone had displaced a brick, and under it
had found a box full of money. Now he remembered
those days like a prisoner recalls his days of
freedom . . .

For three days he remained almost constantly at
the window, moving away only to eat a little barley
bread and goat's cheese. Yes, while his uncle planted
his money under the brick floor, he lived like a poor
shepherd; his house was empty, desolate, without
furniture (he had sold it), even without doors (he
had sold those too), and spiders wove their webs
above the boar's-hide trunk where he kept his poor
mother's wedding and widow's dresses.

To cheer himself he would drink little glasses of
aquavit and return to his window.

From up there he could smell the cakes that the
women were baking for Easter, and see the smoke
rise from the tile roofs. Some nightingales were
already singing in the valley, and little April clouds
passed over the church garden, white as girls' veils
that the wind had carried away from some hedges.

On holy Thursday the widow came out of his
uncle's house and opened the little chapel that was

usually kept closed; and, helped by other women of the neighbourhood, she took down the Christ, laid him on the floor between four candles and four saucers with wheat sprouts, and so fashioned the Sepulchre. Everyone went to the basilica where they celebrated the Mysteries and two true thieves (or at least they were already convicted of theft) were tied on crosses next to Christ. From his window Simone saw his short, fat, bobbing uncle and the tall, dry, stiff widow walking in single file towards the basilica. He went out, but once out on the road he leaned against the wall for a long time, motionless and thoughtful, listening to the distant processional hymns. It was twilight; from a greenish sky the new moon fell upon the violet mountains; the evening star rose and it seemed like they went to meet each other like Mary and Christ do in the village streets on Easter Day.

'In a few minutes the procession will be here,' Simone thought, and he moved; but he walked close to the wall; he was afraid of going through the little chapel in order to enter the garden. He would have to pass by the dead Christ laid out on the floor with the four candles and the four saucers of sprouting wheat.

Suddenly, after reaching his uncle's door, he started. The door was open; someone was in the house and it was useless to go on. He went back and leaned against the wall once more. But who could be in his uncle's house? The servants, farmers and shepherds wouldn't come back until Saturday evening; the priest and the widow were walking behind the procession. He went to the door again, knocked, and called, 'Basila! Basila!'

His voice was lost within the house, already dark, as in a cave. He went in, closed the door, ran up the stairs, crossed the narrow hallway, found the key, opened the door, and he was in his uncle's room. It all seemed like a dream. The window was closed; a candle like those four around the dead Christ burned in front of the image of the holy martyrs. There were so many of them: men, women, old people, children, but they were all looking upwards and their faces were so gentle that Simone was not afraid of them. In the greenish lamplight he bent over and began to feel each brick, one by one, like a mason charged with repairing the floor; but not one of the bricks moved, and he rose and passed a hand over his forehead damp with cold sweat.

He heard the processional hymn and trembled all over. Leaning against his uncle's little bed it moved, creaking and trembling as though caught by the same terror and excitement as the thief. Then Simone looked at the brick where the bed leg had been resting and it seemed to him that the brick had moved. He bent over and prised it up with his fingernails, and in an empty space, buried in dust, he found a little milk can with two thousand lire notes inside.

On Easter Day Father Barca sent widow Basila away, and in a moment the whole town was inundated by a storm of scandal. It was known that the priest was missing many thousands of lire – some said, two, some three, some twenty; and that on Holy Friday evening Basila had left the door of the house open. The brigadier went to the priest's house; the priest did his best to appear unconcerned, but he clapped his hands and said, 'Ah me! Ah me! Ah me!'

On Tuesday the widow's little house was searched, and she was arrested and released the following day. No charge was made against her; but the inhabitants, or rather, the families of the town, were divided, because the men defended Basila by saying that perhaps she had really forgotten about leaving the door open, making it easy for a thief to enter, and the women sneered: 'And in a few minutes the thief made himself at home?'

Then people stopped their murmuring; but everyone looked upon the widow with contempt; no one gave her work any more and she no longer went to church. She lived in poverty in her hovel, and Simone would often see her standing straight in her doorway, pale and sad looking, but with her large green eyes turned upwards like those of the holy martyrs.

Simone paid the forged promissory note and bought back his doors and overcoat. No one was surprised about it, because, like every gambler, he often had these ups and downs of luck, and no one except his creditor knew about the promissory note. What surprised people was to see him so abruptly change his way of living. He no longer kept company with bad women or bad companions, he went to church, he greeted his uncle. But his uncle continued to turn his face the other way when he saw him, and one day when Simone met him and decided to stop him and kiss his hand, not only did he ignore his greeting, but turned his back and walked away.

Simone was stunned. He leaned against the wall and remained riveted there, overcome by an anxious thought. 'He knows!'

Then he went to widow Basila and said to her, 'Do you think you could make bread for me and wash and mend my clothes? You set the price.'

The widow was standing erect before the spent *focolare* combing her hair. The thick, very long, golden chestnut hair made a martyr's halo around her olive face; but when she saw Simone she pulled it over her cheeks and breast like a veil, and lowered and raised her head threateningly, while her green eyes flashed under thick black knitted brows.

'You already have someone to make your bread and wash your things! Get out of here!'

He went away like a whipped dog and returned to lean against the wall.

'She knows!'

He spent his days like that, leaning against the wall, often whittling on his walnut walking stick or a piece of cork or wood, but more often doing nothing. Not even during his worst times had he lived so stupidly. Always before him were the widow's threatening eyes, and he felt an almost physical illness when he thought that Basila had fallen into poverty and bad repute because of him. Some nights he had frightening dreams; the trunk with his mother's clothes seemed like a live boar, and he stared fixedly at the doors he had bought back with *that money.*

Summer passed, and in the autumn he moved from his place against the wall, looking for sun. And from there he could see Basila better – she also sitting in the sun spinning or cooking, barefoot and poor as a slave.

The winter was long and severe. The poor suffered from hunger, and Father Barca and a lady who lived in the neighbourhood sent bread and vegetables to all the poor except the widow. A neighbour with whom Simone had more than once amused himself sent him a leg of mouflon for a Christmas present. He also had a roast pig and a lamb. Thinking that Basila had nothing but potatoes, he tried to send her the mouflon, and was surprised when she didn't reject the gift. Then, for the rest of the winter, seized by a real mania of expiation, he continued to send her presents, often even depriving himself of necessities.

Spring returned. The women again prepared the saucers of wheat sprouts to decorate the tombs. On the eve of Good Friday Simone walked in the procession and when he returned he stood for a while in his usual place against the wall on that warm evening full of whispers. A yellow light could be seen through the crack in Basila's door, and Simone stared strangely at that mysterious light. Suddenly he went over and knocked on the door and asked the woman if she wanted to marry him.

People murmured and then stopped murmuring. After all, Basila was only ten years older than Simone, and was a good housekeeper. In a short time, in fact, the young man's house seemed like a different place – clean, with a fire often burning in the oven, and the courtyard alive with chickens. Simone was seen on his horse again, as when his mother was alive, and everyone said that he had married Basila to spite his uncle.

He was not in love with his wife, but he followed her advice and was happy to be relieved of the weight on his conscience and to have married a wise woman. His wife went to church again and spoke in platitudes, and he felt he had returned to the happy times when his mother was alive and he, still an innocent twenty-year-old, slept in her bed and repeated his prayers after her.

One day, several months after he was married, the woman who had sent him the leg of mouflon called to him as he passed by her door, and asked him to lend her a hundred scudi. He began to laugh.

'If I had a hundred scudi I'd take a trip around the world.'

'I'll pay you interest, Simone Barca! I can pay my debts; I'll give you twenty per cent, too, like the others give you.'

'You've gone crazy, Mallena Porcu!'

'What do you mean, crazy? Tell me that you don't trust me, Simone Barca, but don't insult me. You and your wife have lent money at twenty per cent interest to others. Why shouldn't you give it to me, too? Or is it true what your uncle Father Barca says? That your wife loans the money from a supply she hides from you?'

Simone grew pale, but replied, 'My uncle has become childish, and you are what you are!'

After this he was seen leaning against the wall again as he had done during his bad times. He kept asking himself, 'Why was the door open?' and his thoughts worked continually, digging down, down, through gloomy depths, searching for the truth like a miner searches for gold in the dark bowels of the earth.

'She must have taken a good part of the money and left the door open so people would think some thief came in. Ah, the sly old fox! . . .' he thought angrily. But before giving credence to this thought he wanted to assure himself with his own eyes.

It was once again Good Friday, and Basila had gone to church. Simone waited for that time when it would be easier to go through the whole house; but as much as he searched, through the drawers, in the chest, under the mattresses, he found nothing. Tired of rummaging, he looked around, and in the dusk the trunk that still held his mother's dresses again seemed like a live boar. He tried to open it but could not. Then he remembered that Basila always kept the keys with her. He went down into the kitchen, came back with an axe and began to strike the trunk as though it really were a ferocious boar. The lid broke. Simone knelt down and began going through it; he found the dresses Basila wore as a widow, and from her black hood two, three, many bank notes fell silently, fluttering, red, green, yellow, like dried up leaves from a walnut tree. Among them was a thousand lira bill. He picked it up, looked at it against the candle light and read the name of Father Barca perforated with a pin. Then he began to swear and hit himself on the head. 'But why me? Why me?' he said aloud.

Suddenly a sweet and melancholy dirge like a murmuring in the woods came from the little road. Simone stood listening silently, head bowed, his eyes wide open; and as the procession drew near he began to tremble and perspire just like the time he leaned against his uncle's little bed.

The Treasure

That year farmer Gian Gavino Alivesu sowed his
wheat around the ruins of a church near the sea. It
was rough ground, hard to work, and even though
he had got it for almost nothing, Gian Gavino was
sorry he had taken it.

Every once in a while on those still warm autumn
afternoons, after pulling up some big mastic tree
roots or heaving away rocks, he would straighten up
with his hand on his sweaty back and look at the
green line of the sea, thinking that, after all, hermits
had the best life.

Legend had one of them dying there by the
church ruins, one who had lived a hundred and
seven years ago and who, even then, no one had
seen die; so Gian Gavino, still a young man with a
simple heart, hoed gently at times for fear of disturbing the bones. Yes, he thought bending again over

111

his hoe, a hermit's life is the best. What do hermits do? Nothing. They eat what they find, like birds, they sleep and don't fall into sin; peace on earth and peace in the other world. The rich, for example, also do nothing, it's true; but the sins they commit? If they are goodhearted, God-fearing people, they too end up seeking solitude and poverty, like his namesake, the old lawyer Don Gavino Alivesu (they weren't related), who after studying and spending a lot of money and knowing many distant lands, was now living alone, forever shut up in his house – there it was down on the horizon, white, tall, almost like a bell tower above the broken line of houses in the little village.

In order to see down there better the little farmer stood up again among the rocks and burnt mastic tree roots, with his hand on his back. It was hard work. But still, it's God's commandment to work. However, the sad and sleepy sun had already disappeared behind the red streaks above the coastline, and he thought it was good for him to have a rest too.

He was in no hurry; he didn't want to become rich. What good was wealth? So he could take a wife? Women didn't want him, simple, ugly, and orphaned as he was. If he were rich they would want him for his money, not for love, and it would be sinful anyway. And then women are clever about eating up money. Legend said that the hermit had run away from Spain and come to the solitary coast because of a woman; and also that Don Gavino Alivesu, even though a

112

lawyer, had been badly treated by women. He hated them so much that after he retired to his hill-top castle he didn't want to see them any more, not even in a painting. He received only men, those who went to ask his advice. At first it was opinions and questions about their disputes; then they begged him to act as peacemaker to settle come controversy; then in time he had become the conscience of the little village and everyone ran to him as to a man of God, above human deceitfulness, certain of his truthfulness and above all of his confidential and sure advice. Women also sent their men to him, since they were unable to go there themselves, and the village's sorceress lost nearly all of her customers.

However, Gian Gavino didn't know him, even by sight. He had never needed advice, and he usually turned to God when he needed some little thing. Besides, for some time little had been said about Don Gavino Alivesu. People now had fewer scruples of conscience; also, there was less wrongdoing. You went to America, needed a passport, a letter of good conduct; in order to make your fortune these days you had to be honest.

If Gian Gavino was thinking about the solitary gentleman it was because in his fantasy he saw him next to the hermit of the little church, both sitting on the sea shore, down there among the wave-battered rocks and the diving gulls and sea eagles.

And so, after looking in the direction of the sea again, he took up the hoe he had stuck in the hard soil. As the ground moved he saw something like a large yellow flat seed. He picked it up and looked at it in the palm of his hand and felt his knees buckle and tremble as though he had been given a hard blow on his back. Yes, it was a gold coin.

Everything began to spin around him; the sea went towards the village, the village towards the sea; and in a state of confusion he fell down on his knees and began to dig frantically, with his hands and with his hoe, gathering the money that kept coming up from the ground like a hidden spring. He filled his pockets, he threw the coins down the front of his shirt. Then he put them next to the hole and continued to dig, panting desperately; now, no, he no longer felt his fatigue. He could have spent the rest of his life kneeling in the dusk, with sweat pouring down his cheeks and falling into the bowels of the earth.

But at a certain depth nothing came up any more except some shards of black clay that broke at the touch and turned to powder. Nevertheless he continued searching, putting his arm down as far as it would go, with his chest on the ground, and his desperate face turned westward. When he was convinced there was nothing more, he sat on the pile of earth, with the money between his legs, and like a child began to count it. There were so many pieces, all gold. All he had to do was clean the dirt off and brush a leaf over them to make them shine. Where to put them? He gathered up the clay pieces and tried to make them into a jug. But he immediately

114

realized that he was acting like an idiot and sighed
deeply.

For many days he kept his treasure hidden in his
leather purse. But he was afraid someone might steal
it and so he slept on it, or rather, thinking about
what he had to do, he didn't sleep at all. He didn't
go to the village any more for fear that he would be
tempted to spend a coin and in that way reveal his
secret and expose himself to the danger of having
his treasure taken from him. He was afraid of the
Law. He knew that treasures belonged in part to
the owner of the land where they were found and in
part to the Government. So they would give him a
small part and everyone would laugh at him.

And he was afraid of women – may they burn in
hell; that they would throw themselves on him like
sea eagles pounce on lambs lost in the wilds. And
more than anything he was afraid of his relatives who
lived nearby and who had always taken him for a
simpleton, a good-for-nothing. He wanted to show
them, or rather himself, that he was as clever as the
others, that he was even more clever than the others.
And so he ate little in order to stretch out his provisions longer and not have to go to the village, and
he worked with the leather purse tied across his
shoulders. But one day he came to the end of
his provisions and had to go to the village. It was
then he got the idea of asking Don Gavino Alivesu
for advice.

The old lawyer's house was always open to everyone. An outside stairway led from the solitary, grassy courtyard to the top floor, and Gian Gavino went straight up with his load without knocking. He found himself in a bare room, with a trap door in the wooden ceiling through which he could see the ceiling of the room above. And he stood there looking up with his nose in the air like Giaffà, the simpleton in the Sardinian story, when his mother threw the beans he was eating out of the window. Yes, everyone was received by Don Gavino Alivesu. But how did you find him?

'Ohooo! Anyone here?'

Then a ladder was lowered through the trap door and he climbed up it, staggering with the weight on his shoulders. As soon as he put his head through the trap door, instead of a hermit with a white beard, he saw a still young, plump man, with a black beard framing his bright brown face. He was writing, seated at a table next to an open window: from there you could look over brush land to where Gian Gavino sowed his grain. The sea seemed right there, between one book and another on the table.

But what amazed Gian Gavino most was seeing a tall, strong woman, a pale giantess, who was making the bed, and who, at a signal from the master, went down through the trap door gathering her skirt around her. She was a stranger whom Gian Gavino had seen sometimes on horseback, alone on the road; where she might be going or why he didn't know, because he had never cared about other people's business. And anyway, perhaps Don Gavino Alivesu had changed his opinion about women.

When the solitary man, turning slightly with the pen in his hand, asked him, 'What do you want?' he opened his mouth but was unable to speak. No, he could not. The man before him with pen in hand resembled so many others – the mayor, for example, who was a relative, the doctor, the judge. And why was he writing? To whom was he writing? Gian Gavino remembered going to Nuoro once, to be a witness, and being put up in the house of the godfather of one of his relatives. And in the courtyard that evening he had told a little story to the servants and the girls taking the fresh air. Well, one of these girls, who wrote, had the little story printed on a sheet of paper. And the teacher and the judge had read it and laughed at him, Gian Gavino, and also at her, the daughter of his relative's godfather. No, he was afraid of people who wrote.

'Well, then?' asked the solitary gentleman patiently, looking him in the face with his beautiful, black, lively eyes. 'What do you want?'

'Nothing, excuse me, forgive me for bothering you. I wanted . . . I wanted to ask you, who is that woman?'

He gestured with his head at the trap door, winking a little. And the man laughed like a boy, showing all his white, shining teeth.

'I understand,' he said, turning back to the table.

'Who is she? Who is she?' the winking Gian Gavino insisted.

'As a matter of fact, she's a fine woman. She's a widow and pretty well off. She comes here every once in a while to consult me about a law suit. She comes from good people, but I believe that if she wanted to marry again her relatives wouldn't object. Fine, fine. Do you want me to call her?'

'No, I'll talk to you, if you don't mind . . .'

'Fine, fine. What do you do? Are you a farm manager or a shepherd?'

'A shepherd,' said Gian Gavino.

He didn't know why he was afraid of this man, of those black eyes that caught everything and seemed to penetrate even inside his purse.

'God be with you,' he said hurriedly, backing as far as the trap door. And he went away, but the name of God made him feel sad. He had sinned: he had lied, been suspicious of that charitable man, had pretended interest in a strange woman, a widow who after all had done nothing to him. As he went back down he saw her standing quietly at the bottom of the ladder as though waiting for him, her enormous eyes of a giantess fixed on him. It seemed to him that she had heard everything, and he blushed as he passed by her, barely nodding.

But while Gian Gavino was returning to his solitude, with his load on his shoulders and a thousand anxieties weighing on his heart, he saw her again. Strong, calm, sitting side-saddle on a little red horse, she stared ahead at the coastal road; on reaching Gian Gavino she slowed the horse to a walk and looked down at the young man from her height;

118

and he blushed a second time. Thus they made friends. She spoke well and never laughed. She talked about not being afraid of travelling alone, even at night. If she had to ride at night she dressed as a man, and had once been stopped by bandits; but trusting in God keeps one safe from harm.

'And you,' she asked from above, 'why did you ask about me? What were your intentions?'

'Good intentions. But . . . it's because I saw you on horseback and you didn't seem so tall. I'm too short for you.'

'We're all the same height before God.' She was the first woman to talk to him like that, and he felt his heart pounding, but the palpitation shook him to his shoulder under the hard purse of his treasure and he became suspicious again. Perhaps the woman knew and was courting him for his money.

When they parted he followed her with his sad eyes, and during the restless night he got the idea of hiding his treasure in the crevices of the reef that only sea eagles could reach. There would be time to reclaim it later, if she was really as she seemed and would accept him as a poor man. So he set off. It was a blue autumn night with the moonlight making a long golden serpent on the sea, and at a sheer drop from the cliff the motionless water seemed like milk. Since a child he had known the crevices where the sea eagles made their nests, and it didn't take long to find a suitable one. He left the purse there, but after returning to his hut he staggered around shaking his worried head, uncertain,

119

already remorseful. He could not sleep or rest until dawn when he went back to recover his treasure. Now everything was blue and blood-red in the sea, and under the reef the water was so still that it reflected the shadow of the gulls and eagles in flight.

The lonely man felt dismal amid the calm. He looked everywhere among the crevices, but the sun came up and he still hadn't found his treasure. Finally he thought he saw something that looked like a dead animal floating in the distance, and he realized the truth. The eagles, believing the purse to be an animal, had carried it away and let it drop in the sea.

Gian Gavino went back and began to wait for the woman at least to pass by. But she never came his way again.

The Gold Cross

We were approaching the Christmas season and I had been asked to write a short story for a foreign newspaper and still hadn't found a subject for it.

Then I thought of going to collect some legends (I was still living in Sardinia).

I was acquainted with an elderly man who knew many legends, a tenant on our small farm in the valley; in summer and winter he would come up, bent over his walking stick, with his full *bisaccia* over his shoulder and chest and his beard flowing into it.

He would almost always come late in the evening; the evening star would smile down on us children from the dusky lilac sky. To us the old man seemed like one of the Magi who had taken the wrong road and lost his companions. His *bisaccia* was full of things more precious to us than gold and myrrh: fruit and stories.

121

But he didn't come in the winter, or came rarely, but it wasn't so important to us because he would bring olives, and olives are bitter.

And so I went down there to find him. It is comfortable in the valley in the winter, sheltered as it is; the clouds spread a veil over it like over a cradle. The water is carried off leaving the slopes dry. If the weather is nice it seems like spring; the almond trees flower, deceived by the weather like dreamers, the bindweed blossoms and the olives shine in the grass like purplish pearls.

The little old man lived in a truly romantic hut against a ridge on the sloping olive grove, sheltered by hard sandstone boulders and bushes. He also had a crude cork beehive where beautiful wild cats sat like little tigers.

The sun warms as far as the wall, the olive trees are silvery and the afternoon is so clear on the slopes of the facing mountain that you can see rivulets sparkling and women gathering acorns in the grass.

The old man has spread olives out on the wall to dry and is picking out the damaged ones. He has no desire to talk; solitude and silence have rusted his tongue.

But the servant has brought a good medicine down here to loosen his tongue, and the old man drinks and begins to complain.

'What stories do you want me to tell you? I'm old and now I must talk only to the earth that is calling me. If you want stories look for them in books. You know how to read.'

'Drink some more,' the servant says, she too is
bent over, picking out the bad olives, 'and then tell
us about the time you wanted to get married. Come
on!'

'That's a true story, not a legend; yes, I want to tell
it to you because it happened just at this time, during
the Christmas season.

'I was engaged at twenty. I was very young to take
a wife, but the trouble was that my father was dead
and my mother's health was bad; she had heart
trouble, but was at peace and God-fearing. She told
me: "Get married so when I die you won't be left to
carry life's cross alone, or won't fall into the hands
of the first woman that comes along." ' (We were
thinking: who would want him?) 'I wasn't rich and
couldn't even imagine becoming so; it was enough
that my wife should also be honest and God-fearing.
I thought it over for a long time: who will she be?

'There was a very well-to-do family, father, mother,
and seven children, all hard workers, who went to
mass and confession as God commands. Of these
seven children three were girls – beautiful, tall, slender, with waists like wasps. They always walked with
their eyes downcast, their bodices laced and hands
under their aprons – not like you girls today, with
eyes that seem to devour people. My mother
requested the youngest for me and I was well
received. At Christmas I was to give the gift that
would firmly commit me to marrying her, as is the
custom, and her accepting it meant she would marry
me. And again I thought about this gift a long time

with my mother. Sitting on either side of the *focolare* she and I were always discussing whether this gift should be a gold piece or an embroidered handkerchief or a ring. At last my mother said, "Listen, son, since my days are numbered and every step takes me further from the things of this world, take my gold cross and give it to her."

'And she gave it to me, with the mother-of-pearl rosary attached to it. But as she gave it to me her eyes shone with tears and her mouth gasped open because of her heart trouble; I felt so sorry for her I started to give it back, but she couldn't talk and simply put out her hand to push mine away.

'I wrapped the rosary and cross in one handkerchief inside another, and kept them in my pocket for three days as a kind of relic; every once in a while I would touch them, for fear of losing them, and I felt – I don't know why – my heart swell with love, but also with a strange anxiety.

'So on Christmas Eve I went to my betrothed. The men engaged to the two other sisters were also there and the crowded kitchen seemed like, and was, a festive place. However, everyone was solemn because my future father- and mother-in-law, with their calm but imposing air, inspired respect like saints on the altar. The girls went back and forth with eyes downcast, serving wine and sweets to the young men, responding quietly to their compliments without smiling.

'I wasn't uncomfortable in such a place because I was a serious young man, a fatherless child used to

124

giving serious consideration to the things of life; it was enough for me to look at my fiancée every once in a while. And, when her father and mother turned their backs, if she would quickly raise her eyes to look at me it seemed like the sky opened up, and the kitchen – full of in-laws, engaged couples, the brothers skinning goats for supper – seemed to me the Heavenly Court with God, the Saints and Angels. How happy I was that evening! I've never been so happy. Except that I was anxiously waiting for the time after mass to give my fiancée the gift and so bind myself to her.

'And then someone knocked on the big door to the courtyard. One of the brothers went to open it and came back followed by a tall stranger with a little *bisaccia* over his shoulder and a cattle prod in his hand for a walking stick.

'I watched him closely as he silently came forward, shod as he was in soft shoes without heels like they wear in Oliena. At first he seemed very old to me, with his short white beard and clear eyes; but then I could see that he was young, blondish, tired as though he had come from a town far away.

'None of us knew him and even the women looked at him curiously; but everyone believed him to be a friend of the head of the family because the latter greeted him cordially. "Sit down," he said, "where do you come from?"

'The stranger sat down amidst us without removing his *bisaccia*, the prod on his knees, his feet towards the fire. He looked at each of us one by one, smiling casually, as if we were old acquaintances.

' "I come from far away; I'm just passing through," he said in a voice even calmer than my father-in-law's. "It was a good thing I came to give you my greetings, since you are having a celebration."

' "Yes, we're celebrating, as you see. The girls are engaged. Here are their clever future husbands – handsome and strong as lions. We lack nothing."

' "Nothing at all!" said the young men, poking each other with their elbows and laughing. After so much seriousness even the girls seemed to be overcome by a feeling of exaggerated gaiety; they also laughed a lot, and I laughed too, and so did the in-laws. It seemed to be something catching, going from one to another. Only the stranger remained calm, looking at us like a boy, neither surprised nor offended.

'Finally, when everyone became serious again he said to the women: "Once many years ago I passed through this town and happened to go to a house where there were engaged couples. And they were equally happy; except that one promised bride looked at me often and when I went away she followed me as far as the door and said, 'You are my true husband. I was waiting for you; stay and give me a gift.' I gave her a gift and, even though I went away and she married another, I was the real groom and her son will bring to you, you brides-to-be, the gift that I gave her, and you will pass it on to your sons for their brides."

126

'We looked at each other without laughing or smiling any more. The man seemed odd, almost crazy, and yet after the happiness it awoke in us a strange feeling, almost of fear.

'The mother-in-law asked, "Please – what was your gift?"

' "A gold cross."

'Then I felt a chill run down my back. The son of the stranger's girlfriend could only be me. Only I had my mother's gold cross to give to my bride. I didn't open my mouth, but from that moment I felt like my head was wrapped in a veil. I could see, but confusedly, and my ears were buzzing. I could no longer distinguish the words the stranger, my future mother-in-law and the young people were exchanging.

'I felt a great sorrow, a back-breaking weight, as if the gold cross inside my pocket had suddenly become a great rock bearing down on me.

'Then after the stranger had warmed his feet he went away – tall, silent, with his prod in his hand and his *bisaccia* over his shoulder.

' "Who was he?" the mother-in-law asked.

' "Who knows?" the father-in-law replied. "I've never met him, but he looked familiar. Yes, I must have seen him many years ago, maybe when he came secretly to visit his girlfriend."

'I remained silent. Again everyone was composed, serious, grave. The girls went back and forth preparing supper, but my fiancée, pale, with eyes downcast, didn't look at me any more. My heart was pounding, and through that veil wrapped around my head I seemed to see the eyes of the old and young people turn towards me every once in a while with suspicion.

'It was like that until time to go to mass; we got up, but feeling still more weighed down, I staggered under my weight and stumbled like a drunk. We went in a row, the women in front, the men behind. Arriving at the church we mixed with the crowd, and I gradually backed up as far as the baptistry, as far as the door, as far as the entrance . . . and there I turned my back on the house of God and ran like I was pursued by demons. I went like a crazy man, running here and there until dawn. At daybreak I went home. My mother was already up; she was lighting the fire and seemed calm but pale, as though she had been awake all night.

'Seeing me so distraught she thought I was drunk and she spread out the mat for me to lie down. All she said was, "You've made a bad impression, dear son!"

'I threw myself down, I bit the mat. Then I got on my knees, took out the gold cross, twisted it and the rosary broke, scattering the beads all over the floor in every direction but towards me. They seemed frightened of me. My mother began to pant. Taking pity I told her everything.

' "What could I do?" I shouted. "The girlfriend of the unknown man, the stranger, was you. Could I give your cross to my fiancée? Everyone was watching me, guessing the truth. I ran away out of shame."

'My mother calmed down. She gathered the beads

128

in her apron and began restringing them. She waited until I was quiet, then she said, "Why couldn't the other two be the sons of the stranger's girlfriend?"

' "Because they had gold pieces to give to their brides, not crosses . . ."

' "Money also has its cross," she said. "Listen to me. A stranger goes to all the brides' houses to give them a cross. Do you think those three girls didn't go after him last night also? Yes, they too have a cross and their sons will be his sons. How simple you are!" she said seeing my astonishment. "Don't you believe in God? Yes, you believe in God and in Christ, and you know that Christ is not dead. He lives for ever, He's in the world with us, and He goes around to the houses blessing and multiplying the loaves of bread to whomever gives Him charity. He blesses and makes the water of those with a good heart as sweet as wine; and to all brides He gives a cross – a cross of gold, yes, but a cross! It was He, and you, simpleton, you didn't recognize Him!"

'And so the cross,' the old man concluded, 'was mine, all mine!'

Drama

Although all the men were in town during the final weeks of Lent to fulfil their Easter duties, beautiful Ilaria's *rivendita* was deserted, because it was a time of penance and no one dared get drunk.

Ilaria herself would have scrupulously objected if it were any other way, and yet she remained waiting in the usual place, black and stiff as a widow sitting in front of the large fireplace whose red-gleaming flame gave the room the colour of an ancient tavern. That is, she stayed there all day; only at night did she retire to her adjoining bedroom to sleep – and no one was familiar with her bedroom. However, all the men who came to the wine shop knew the corner of the fireplace where they sidled up to warm their rough hands or to pick up a live coal in their fingers to light their pipes – or still better, to try to court Ilaria. But though the ember let itself be taken, Ilaria was less touchable than live coals. In her taciturnity she wouldn't even reply to the men's proposals; she would only look at them with her large, gloomy green eyes, her pale face framed by a square black cloth fastened under her chin with a silver chain. She would look at them, sad and threatening, and then point to the fireplace. On the black wood frame, scratched with the point of a pocket knife, were twelve notches: twelve years her husband had been paying the penalty for killing the man who had boasted of being her lover.

It was during this time, towards Easter, that she always cut the mark on the fireplace; and reading (with some difficulty) the Holy Week book she would unite her suffering with Christ's. Yes, those had been terrible weeks, then three days of death during the deliberation and sentencing of her husband. Then she also awoke, but her sepulcre stone had not moved.

Life blazed around her in the shouts, gaiety, drunkenness and violent anger of the men who frequented her wine shop, but she was as silent as a dead woman, firmly in her place at the back. From the always open door she saw only the white line of the main road bordered by a grassy ridge, above which pasturing horses and cows slowly passed head down against the desolate background of the sky. At times the silence and the stillness around gave her the impression that everything – the distant world heavy with her husband's pain, and the nearby world heavy with her pain – everything was a dream, a quiet tomb.

And yet, after all, in this apparent death she did nothing but wait. One day, therefore, towards the end of Lent, while she was dozing with the book in her hands, a man – almost an adolescent, tall, supple as a woman – looked in from the doorway, poking his head in cautiously like someone escaping from danger and looking for refuge.

Ilaria's eyes opened wide, but she thought she was still dreaming. The man entered, stooping at the doorway he was so tall, and he went to sit at the table at the back next to the violet-coloured barrels. He didn't ask for anything. He put his elbows on the table, his brown face in his white hands, and began to stare at Ilaria, smiling at her, but also laughing at her, with his black shining eyes behind his fingers. She looked at him, too, and the chain under her chin trembled from emotion. Finally she got up and went to the table.

'What's your order, Don Mattia?'

'Give me wine from Oliena, if you have it.'

While he drank she went back to her place and stirred the fire. Her heart was pounding. She thought she knew why the man had come and was waiting for him to talk.

In fact, excited by the wine, he was the first to speak.

'Well, then, Ilaria, what are you thinking? I already know. You think that my wife and mother-in-law have sent me. You think that they have gone to confession, and that the confessor has said to them: "All right then, be forgiving, women, grant that poor woman's

desire. Sign the request for her husband's pardon."
Yes, Ilaria, the priest did come to us one day and
brought his ambassador and said: "Ilaria is sure to
obtain the pardon for her husband if the request is
signed by the widow and daughter of the victim."
Yes, perhaps that's the way it is, perhaps it can really
be obtained . . . And so, do you think those women
will agree?'

Ilaria had turned completely on her stool, rigid,
with her large pleading eyes full of burning light.
The man was smiling cruelly, his teeth violet from
the thick wine he had drunk.

'Yes, go and try to see them; they will strangle you.
You know what my mother-in-law said? That you had
provoked the dead man. You, goodlooking – because
he was rich, and a rich man, even if old and married,
always tempts a tavern mistress . . . if only to use as a
lure to her place.'

While he talked Ilaria's pupils dilated as though
from physical pain. She did not reply. She turned
back to the fireplace and slumped down beside it,
though not poking it now. Her foolish hope had
collapsed. Her enemies were unforgiving, and
nothing was more important to her in the whole
world. She let the man, more and more drunk, do
the talking.

Nothing shook her any more: the slander, the hate,
the threats of her enemies, not even her curiosity to
know why Don Mattia, after two years of marriage,
on orders from his wife and mother-in-law never to

put his foot in the tavern, should suddenly come and entertain himself by tormenting her.

However, after making some vague allusions to the years when he had come to the tavern as a ruined young gentleman with his friends because he didn't know where else to go, he grew silent, and only the soft sound of the wine pouring from the bottle into the glass broke the silence from time to time. And the silence was such that he heard a little boy whistle far away, behind the hill, and it seemed that the world ended there, at the row of grey rue bushes mixing with the bright March clouds.

Ilaria was almost afraid to turn around. She again had the impression of a dream. She was reading but understood the words of the book less now than ever. Finally someone arrived. It was a shepherd, an unrepentant drunk who had taken communion a few hours earlier, but who could not leave without making a visit to Ilaria's.

He seemed frightened too by the sight of Don Mattia. He came in on tiptoe and squatted on his heels in front of the fire; turning towards Ilaria he winked.

'Now, oh, when those women find out they are going to kill me!' Don Mattia went on.

Ilaria looked at him without speaking.

'They will die of anger, with their pride they will split like a ripe pomegranite.'

Silence from Ilaria. The shepherd spoke up, but in hushed tones: 'Because he is here out of spite. He has quarrelled with his mother-in-law and his wife.

Everyone knows it. He has quarrelled with them because they keep him under their fist like their servant . . . of course, they are rich; he sponges off them.'

Ilaria turned to see if Don Mattia was listening. Don Mattia, with his face in his hands, his eyes closed, was sleeping. The tragic peace of a man who has revenged himself and rests after the vendetta; it smoothed his fine features but also gave him a deathly aspect. Ilaria, who had known him as a child, an orphan abandoned to the care of poor relatives, then had seen him as a lazy adolescent becoming suddenly rich and a slave, looked at him a moment with pity; then she turned towards the fire and resumed her hard, steady look.

II

Don Mattia's frequent visits soon began to worry her. He was always there, speaking badly of his mother-in-law with his old friends and even with the roughest customers. Once Easter had passed, the wine shop was full of people, especially on Saturday evenings and Sundays.

He was always there, even in the morning, and some curious women went by the main road deliberately just to look inside the wine shop.

One day the priest came to see Ilaria.

'You know that it's a scandal. The whole town says it was you who enticed Mattia, that you sent for him and keep him here and get him drunk because those women haven't signed the request. What about it, what are you thinking, Ilaria? You haven't been to confession.'

Ilaria gritted her teeth to keep from swearing; the chain trembled under her chin.

'Ilaria,' said the priest, patting her knees kindly, 'we know it's not true: I, you and he, we know it, and perhaps even some other people who say it's true knowing they lie. All right then, you know: truth's not important, but appearance is. Send Mattia away so he can go back home and no longer be spiteful. He is in love with his wife and comes here to dull his senses.'

Ilaria asked him, 'Have those women sent you?'

'Yes,' the priest confessed.

'Well, listen then: tell them to give me their signature on the request and I'll send Don Mattia away from the wine shop.'

The negotiations went on for several days. Finally the priest brought the signed paper.

That very evening Mattia lingered in the wine shop, drinking and gambling; however, he was preoccupied, and even after the others had gone away he stayed on, as pale and troubled as that day of his first visit.

It was late: the large moon rose behind the bushes on the ridge and seemed to look sneeringly into the wine shop. Ilaria stood up and leaned her hands on the table.

'Don Mattia, I want to ask you a favour: go away

136

and never come back. People are talking and say that I enticed you here. I hope my husband will come back soon. Go away. Have pity on me.'

'My mother-in-law is slandering you, I know,' the man said. 'So much the better.'

'What do you mean, better? What have I done to you, Don Mattia, for you to allow her to slander me?'

'You haven't done anything to me. It's her, hang her, who has wronged me. But I've sworn to make her die of a broken heart and so she will!'

'Don Mattia! You're the evil one! You're a lazy, vicious man.'

'Oh, oh!' he said, surprised by her courage. Then he began to laugh. 'I know that they've signed the request, in order to send me away. But my wife's signature isn't valid without mine. Oh, well, to show you I'm not vicious like you say, I'll sign. Give me the paper.'

Ilaria gave it to him. As he looked at the paper he said, 'Yes, your husband has paid half the penalty, and thanks to good behaviour he will probably be pardoned. He was drunk when he committed the crime, he was very young, and you were also young, Ilaria. How old were you?'

'Twenty, Don Mattia,' she said, placing the ink in front of him; but first with surprise and then with terror she saw the man put the request in his pocket without signing it.

'Actually, you're right, Ilaria. If he comes back he

could kill me. Maybe that's what my mother-in-law wants.'

Then Ilaria took her head in her hands, under the black mantle; she seemed to go crazy. She fell on her knees, shrieked, stretched out her shaking arms.

'Give me the paper! Give me the paper!'

He got up to close the door. While she stood leaning on the table he returned to his place and said to her sadly: 'Listen, Ilaria, listen; don't shout, turn around, don't be afraid. I'll give you the request, or rather, I'll send it and recommend it to whomever I can. I can hurt you but I don't want to. Look at me. Don't you see I am an unfortunate man, worse off than you?'

'But what do you want from me?' she shouted, turning to look at him.

'Come here next to me and I'll tell you.'

And very slowly, as though under a spell, she went around the table, bent over him and, crying, allowed him to kiss her.

III

But a year passed before he kept his word. The paper remained in his pocket. Ilaria could have stolen it and sent it off, but she didn't. At first it was because of scruples of conscience: she didn't want to make use of the signatures since not only had she not kept her part of the bargain, but she was tied to the man with the bond of sin.

The priest came back to see her. She bowed her head and asked, 'What can I do?'

A year later, near Easter time, she made the thirteenth mark on the fireplace – then started as though from a sudden revelation. She realized that she had always been waiting; but now she was afraid for time to pass.

One day Mattia sat at the table, pale and troubled as the first evening when Ilaria had kissed him.

'Do you know that my mother-in-law is dying? The heartaches I gave her are killing her.'

Ilaria did not reply. She knew it.

'Within days, maybe even tomorrow, as soon as she dies, I'll become the head of the family. I mustn't come here any more; I must take my place, remember to be a man, a good Christian. My wife also suffers, and she is good to me now, she seems like another person. Ilaria, we must be good in this world, otherwise everything is lost.'

She did not reply. She knew it.

'Ilaria,' he said quietly, bending closer to look at the wine-stained table, 'I'll send the request for pardon and a deputy will talk to the minister. Are you happy?'

She bent over, holding her head in her hands under her cloak like the other time.

'Ah, Mattia! Wretched man! Now you do it, now?'

But he was struck senseless. He seemed to be sleeping like that first day when he came to her to get drunk.

'Mattia, I can't let you go now. Mattia, he will kill you if he comes back!'

'I don't care. If he kills me it means that I must pay for my sin.'

'Mattia, give me the paper! I'll send it myself.'

She held out her trembling arms, pleading like on that other evening. But he quickly raised his eyes and smiled briefly, cruelly. Then he lowered his head.

'Ilaria, I've already sent it.'

The First Trip

Old as she was, and after travelling halfway round
the world – to Lourdes on a pilgrimage, to Barcelona
for business, to Rome to testify in a famous trial –
Donna Itria still remembered her first trip: a memory
lost in the night of time.

'In the night of time' was the expression she used
every time she came to Nuoro as a guest in our house
and spoke about her first trip. And she came often
because she had many lawsuits to take care of. She
spoke well and defended her case in court like a
lawyer. She was strong. She came by horse, sitting
sidesaddle like an amazon, followed by a servant she
never spoke to unless it was to criticize him for something. The man was patient and did not reply; but
as soon as he saw Donna Itria turn her back he
tapped a dark index finger on his forehead to tell
us that his mistress was crazy.

Once, however, she treated him so badly that he criticized her openly. Only a few words: 'It's enough to say that she let her husband die in an insane asylum.'

Donna Itria despised men. When she found out that I was to be married she came just to bring me a gift and to repeat her well-known story about her first trip, so that I might receive some lesson from it.

'In the night of time, you know, but when men had already acquired cunning. Perhaps women didn't yet have it, at least I didn't. But who would have taught me? My father and mother were dead, my sister Bonaria was so crippled she never left the house; the grandfather we lived with was simple in the old-fashioned way, so simple and so old-fashioned that he made a will leaving four-fifths of his land to Bonaria – that is, the hill of Sant' Antoni 'e Mare, that a family could make a living from only as an asphodel pasture. And do you know why he did this? Because, he said, I had hills and *tancas* in my eyes, and Bonaria would never be able to find a husband. I didn't complain; I had slender legs and felt I could go to the ends of the world in search of fortune and happiness. And in fact that year I went with my newly married aunt and uncle on their honeymoon to San Giovanni di Mores: fifteen hours of travel in a stagecoach.

'In the night of time – yes, it was still night when we left – I was happy but also full of remorse because poor Bonaria was home. But I thought about bringing her a nice gift, a silver pin box or a pair of blue

142

stockings like they were beginning to wear. And I really would bring her a nice gift, you'll see! My heart was pounding (do you know how old I was? fifteen or sixteen!) because when I left the house on tiptoe in order not to wake up Bonaria, and crossed the sleeping town, I seemed to hear a thousand sounds, as if to say that the whole world were going to a festival, singing and playing instruments. And here was the stagecoach large as a small house moving under an arch of stars. We were alone in it, my aunt and uncle under the same large cape to keep close to each other, I with my shawl embroidered with geraniums.

'My uncle said, "Put out those lanterns, Itria!" Imagine if I had the desire to sleep. The whole earth trembled and roared around me and we seemed to be running up a mountain with so many stars looking down upon me from between the black holm-oak and the sea at the end of the road.

'We smelled the sea, in fact, and my uncle said, "Do you know where we are now, Itria? On the hill of Sant' Antonio. Daybreak and sunrise will come before we cross it. However, your descendants will enjoy it, Itrié; you, however, have those fawn's legs."

'And he held me as though I were a precious thing. I laughed and my uncle said, "She'll have land, this one here."

'And so we arrived at the road keeper's house and in the silence of the early morning a voice strong but as fresh as a nightingale shouted, "Don't doubt it, Pancraziu, I'll be comfortable. A slim man like me is comfortable anywhere!"

'In fact as soon as he was inside, the new traveller filled the stagecoach with his baskets and *bisacce*, and he sat with his legs stretched out as though he were in his own house. I forgot – he had a large coat of coarse wool, quilted all over, and every once in a while he shook the hem, tossing it between his legs without taking his hands from his pockets. But he was handsome. I had never seen such a handsome man: tall, his head a little bent over in order not to touch the top of the stagecoach. Good-looking men were forgiven everything at that time, too. He paid no attention to me and began to talk with my aunt and uncle. He spoke loudly, jestingly.

' "Are you going to the festival? Eh, they say it will be a big one this year. A good amount of everything. The dogs' leashes will be made of sausages."

'My uncle looked at him seriously, and my aunt smiled at me. The traveller took us for some poor people who were perhaps going to the festival to keep a vow. He stuck his head out the window; the sun was rising and the black and golden mountains appeared behind the green valley. We were going uphill and could see rows of pear trees loaded with fruit alongside the road. It was September. The young man looked at the pear trees and said, "This year we planted almost two thousand of them in our *tancas* at Ottana. You've probably heard of the *tancas* of the Rector, my uncle."

'My aunt looked at me and smiled.

144

' "And this land is ours and that is ours. Yes, this year hasn't been bad; we've had a thousand quarts of almonds. My cousin Ascanio Piras, the nephew of the superintendent, you've probably heard him mentioned . . ."

'Yes, my uncle had heard of them: powerful, important people, but the traveller's boasting must have gone against him because he said, "Yes, I know Ascanio Piras: he has rented a piece of Sant' Antoni 'e Mare that this girl's grandfather owns."

'The young man gave a jump and turned to me as though looking at a marvel. I've never forgotten that look.

'And he began to talk and joke with me. He asked me how old I was and if I were married.

' "She's only a girl! Can't you tell she's fifteen years old?" my uncle said.

' "She looks older; she's well developed," said the young man looking me over from head to foot. And I felt as hot as if I were next to a fire under his scrutiny. After all he was the first man so tall and good looking to sit next to me and speak so kindly to me. Every time the stagecoach stopped other people got on, and he pushed closer to me each time.

'We ate and drank together. He asked me if I danced, then he said that he would come to our town's festival and that he would give me a horse. If he spoke about something he owned and I said it must be nice he would immediately reply: "I'll give it to you."

145

'My aunt watched me and smiled. And so night fell and we ate together again. My aunt didn't feel well and my uncle took her outside next to the driver so she could breathe the fresh air. I saw them through the window, wrapped in the same large cape, and I felt a great awe but also a great pleasure at being left alone beside the young man. He had not moved from his place and an old man, remaining in the stagecoach after all the others got off at the last station, was stretched out asleep. It was a cool evening in September and again many stars looked down from the dark heights and the smell of mastic trees reached us.

'I was silent and so was the young man. He only asked, "Are you cold?" And he took his great coat and spread it over my knees, pulling an edge over his own. I wanted to protest, but I was trembling all over and couldn't open my mouth. And like this we reached our destination. I didn't close my eyes in our host's house all night. I wanted to die I was so happy – the trip, the meeting, the young man's love all seemed like a dream. And as soon as I got up I saw him there at the end of the road like the sun. And so we went together to the festival and danced and came back together. And when he left he promised to come to our village festival in October.

'I waited a year and a month. Finally his uncle the Rector came. I remember he was a priest so fat that the horse was sweating under him: a priest that seemed like a bishop with silk hose and silver buckles. Well, he asked for the hand of Bonaria for his nephew! Because you should know that our grandfather had died in the meantime and she had inherited the hill of Sant' Antonio. I was practically destitute: what good did my slender legs do me?'

The Usurer

The usurer was dying and the women sent for the priest so that he could make his confession.

The usurer had always been a good Christian; every year he made his Easter duty and was often seen kneeling in church on the poor people's bench, with his grieving eyes turned to the large Crucifix above the altar. He seemed to be reproaching Christ for making him follow that occupation. Furthermore he had taken into his house (making them leave their own town) some poor, proud, already elderly nieces who had not found husbands because those wanting them were wild young men or from bad families. They wanted gentlemen on the decline or young men from good families, who, even though they borrowed from the usurer, looked down on them because of their connection.

The old priest went to the usurer's house towards

evening after he had made his rounds of the other sick. He was in no hurry, even walking more slowly than usual, leaning on his large shepherd's stick. When he went up the usurer's stairs he stopped wearily at every step and, face downward, made a grimace of disgust.

The house was shabby, dark; an old house with stairs going up and down from every doorway, low ceilings, creaking wooden floors. The torrid heat of that August evening made it even more wretched. Neither did the bedroom furniture reflect the fabulous riches attributed to the usurer. It was still, in other words, the humble dwelling of an orphaned girl from a good family in decline. Forty years ago the usurer had arrived in the little village with two or three pieces of linen and scarlet cloth on his shoulders and a tape measure in his hand like the travelling salesman he was. He had rented a little room overlooking the road for a few days, that is, as long as the feast of the village patron lasted, and there, in that house, he had remained for the rest of his life.

The old priest knew the bedroom well. It belonged to the former owner. The wooden bed, with its yellow and black wool cover embroidered like a tapestry and its red percale pillow cases, was the same one he had blessed so many times on Holy Saturday on his rounds of the village houses. There was the same wardrobe that Alessandra Madau would take money from to put in the holy water bucket and the same chest she took the yellow cake from that she put in the *bisaccia* held by the sexton. But as he drew near the sick man the priest remembered that Alessandra Madau had not died there on her virginal bed. Going from travelling salesman to home owner, the usurer had chased her off and put himself in the noble bed, like an owl in a dove's nest. And he certainly gave the impression of an owl with his perfect usurer's face: hook nose and round, protruding eyes in his pale face, white rumpled hair on the red pillow, which the light from an old copper lantern hanging on the bedpost gave the colour of coagulated blood.

He had a high fever, but easily recognized the priest and immediately stretched out his hand as though asking for help. Little by little his face changed expression as the priest talked to him and squeezed his hand warmly. His half-closed eyes became long, almost sweet. His lips over still sound teeth got back a little colour; his composed white face seemed like a marble mask. Strange thing: he seemed like another person, almost young, almost handsome.

The priest looked at him without letting go of his thin wrist, inside which a single tumultuous and burning vein seemed to pulse. And the priest's suspicions and harsh judgements vanished as though carried away by that wave of deathly fever.

After his confession the usurer continued to grasp the priest's hand tightly. It seemed as though he was afraid to let him go or that he still wanted to tell him something.

From time to time he would raise his white head

150

a little from the red pillow and look towards the wardrobe by a window where some flies, deceived by the orange light of the rising moon, still fluttered against the glass.

The priest was perspiring from the hot stuffiness of the closed room and from the warmth pouring over him from the sick man's hand. Suddenly he felt dizzy and as though he had a fever himself; he felt his sweat grow icy. A door of the wardrobe creaked open and from inside, like a ghost, it appeared: a woman with her back to the room in a black pleated skirt, a little jacket, a fringed kerchief falling to her shoulders. Alessandra Madau as she had been seen on feast days when she went to church with measured steps, as calm and composed as a noble lady.

A tremor began shaking the sick man; his face turned ugly, squeezing up like a newborn that wanted to cry and still didn't know how; and a slight moan, an inhuman lament resembling the door creak issued from his clenched teeth. For a few moments he struggled against this agitation which appeared to cause him such anguish and humiliation. Then he was overcome. Tears bathed his face, ran into his mouth and ears. His mouth opened and the priest heard him moan senseless words.

'You are there . . . you are still there! . . . why don't you go away? Go away, go away . . . I'm tired, I can't take any more.'

Then he grew silent, calmed down. He passed his hands over his face, drying his tears, patting his forehead, cheeks, mouth for a while as though putting his disturbed features back into place. He was not successful, however, as his fingers still trembled.

In the meantime, to put an end to the cause of such pain, the priest rose and pushed the door with his walking stick, almost as though it were too repellent to touch with his hand. However, the door continued to open, to repeat the creaking; and to show its solidarity, the other door opened also, with a different creak, mockingly. The priest then pushed them both with his hands, but as soon as he let go they opened again, one after the other. They seemed to enjoy being disobedient. Seized by curiosity, he had a better look inside the wardrobe. He only smelled the strong odour of camphor and only saw that woman's costume hung with such care that it seemed to be worn by a human body.

He finally managed to close the doors which, to tell the truth, no longer had hooks or a lock, and he also gave them a light tap with his walking stick to punish them. Then he turned back to the bed, bending over to take leave of the usurer.

However, the latter grabbed his hand again, holding it tightly.

His eyes were pleading. What was it he wanted? Had he so much fear and remorse?

'Now calm down! What do you want? Come on, make your peace with God.'

'I've made my peace with Him,' the sick man murmured. Suddenly he sat up and slid out of bed.

The priest felt him leaning against him naked, scrawny, trembling, hot, and he offered him support and repressed a cry so as not to frighten the women in the next room.

'What now . . . what now?'

'Take me,' the sick man begged; and rather than leading him, the priest let himself be pushed by the old man towards the wardrobe.

At the vibration of their steps the doors opened again, and the usurer, while steadying himself with one hand on the priest, took the hem of the skirt with the other and kissed it. Then he passed it over his face, falling on his knees and striking his forehead against the wardrobe. It seemed like he wanted to die like that, at the feet of the phantom.

The priest pulled him up in his arms and, perspiring, with a sense of repugnance and almost terror, and also with a certain anger, he slowly led him back to bed and settled him in as well as he could.

The wardrobe remained open; and it was now his turn to look, to think, to try to relive a time long ago. Following the thread of his thoughts he finally asked, with ill-concealed curiosity: 'What went on between the two of you?'

The usurer, with his head once again sunk into the red pillow, had closed his eyes and seemed tranquil, now at peace with everyone.

'We are before the world of truth,' he murmured. 'She was my lover, yes. Lover, yes. Wife, no. She didn't want it. She was ashamed of me. I was a salesman coming with pieces of cloth on my back . . . and she was a lady! I gave her money, and out of pride she paid me interest. Then the quarrels began.

She was ashamed of me. Lover, yes; wife no. Then she insulted me. I told her: I'll reduce you to a poor woman, a beggar, and then you'll have to marry me. It was she who went away; and the more needy she became the more she despised me. Then she didn't want to see me any more. I hoped she would come back. I kept the wedding dress ready. Then she died. That's how it happened and no one knew about it. But I . . . I have always been the same person and she has always been the mistress here . . .

When he went away, the priest closed the wardrobe again; but the doors reopened immediately, one after the other, and the odour of camphor came through as through a door opened on to the garden of the dead.

Witchcraft

War, drought or famine didn't hurt the business of Compare Diegu, the cobbler-sorcerer. People still needed shoes and, indeed, had special need of supernatural help. Therefore, on that night, a truly legendary night with black clouds, wind and mysterious sounds, a large, hooded figure pushed open Compare Diegu's door, entered, closed it and leaned against a wall in a corner of the hovel where the bald little cobbler was still working. Compare Diegu didn't stop working even though his heart jumped with pleasure when he recognized the hooded figure as Compare Zecchino Pons. The wealthy property owner had never before deigned to visit, though he lived just across the road.

It is true that rich Zecchino Pons was slightly drunk, as he usually was at that hour of the evening: something that caused his large flabby body to stoop a bit, even if it didn't keep him from preserving the serious face of a wise man, or from speaking with a haughty dignity.

'Well, Compare Diegu, how's business? All right, blast you. I saw Mariapaska leaving here today, and a short time ago a black bird that looked like a priest to me . . . And then,' he started up again after a moment of silence, while Compare Diegu continued to bend over an old shoe propped on the leather apron covering his knee, 'then I said to myself: Zecchino Pons, since girls from good families and priests go there, you might as well go to the sorcerer too. Well, I have ready cash, not pounds of fat or sacks of potatoes. When something is done for me, done for Zecchino Pons, ready cash flows. Oh, it means doing it well: a spell that will make a ferocious animal powerless and harmless. It's good for everyone. It's a charitable act. You know I'm a good man. Who has Zecchino Pons ever harmed? Always good, with my right hand and my left. I don't even have a license to carry a gun, because anyone who doesn't know how to defend himself with the hands God gave him won't find weapons that can defend him. And is my wife not a saint? She's there in the house like Maria in her niche. Who would Barbara Pons harm? Not even a fly. We have no children of our own, but all the town's poor are our children. Everyone can see I drink quite a bit of wine. And what does it matter to you?' he shouted threateningly at Compare Diegu who was silently smiling at his shoe. 'It's wine from my own vineyard. So why should I ruin my life and

156

damn my soul because that ferocious animal of a Nicolao, my next-door neighbour, blast him, has sworn to have me sent to prison in this life and to hell in the next?'

The shoemaker lifted his head slightly. He understood. And he was already thinking which Bible verses were needed to cast a spell on the unfortunate Nicolao; but for scruples of conscience he asked softly, 'Are you sure he wants this for you?'

'Sure, sure as can be. This is how it went,' replied the other, counting on his large fingers. 'We got on all right until November. Nicolao often worked for me and my wife and his little urchins were always at my house. They ate from my larder like the famished dogs that they are. In November, remember, those rains came that made half the world a lake. Well then, Nicolao's wife closes the hole of the water drain going from my courtyard to hers. I should drown, not her, you understand! But the law is the law, and when I come back home I find my wife with the house flooded. She was trembling like the little hen that she is, my wife, instead of taking care of it, and the servant, whose name is Ausilia [Helpful] as well, instead of giving a hand was hiding in the woodshed, lazy as she is, because she thought it was the Flood. Then what did I have to do, can you tell me? Not only did I reopen the hole but I made another three in the wall, and emptied the well that was full to the brim. You can surely remember how Nicolao's wife carried on. He kept quiet inside the house, but that same night he tore up all the plants in my garden, and then he poisoned my dog, and after that he shortened the ears of my horse, and no later than yesterday cut the hocks of my oxen in the pasture. All this silently, like the devil, without leaving a trace. I don't even see him any more, and his wife yells when she sees me and says if I dare accuse her husband she will go to the police immediately and charge me with slander.

'And now, since there is no justice in this world, now, I say to myself, let's go to Compare Diegu, let's resort to the devil. If it's true that you cast spells, well, cast one that ties the hands of that wrongdoer and keeps him from damaging my soul. I've lived sixty years without sinning, why should I start now?'

The cobbler was quite relieved, putting the shoe on the black table where a little oil lamp was burning. His yellow face with two thin moustaches, one longer than the other, had a truly diabolical expression. He repeated softly, 'Zecchino Pons, are you certain it's your neighbour who has done these things? Can you be sure in your own conscience?'

The man hesitated a moment. He stooped over further. He seemed to be looking inside himself.

'I have no enemies. I can promise you he's the one. And in order not to have scruples, if you aren't a cheat also and the charm is successful, you'll see who Zecchino Pons is. I'll think of everything to help your family, providing my soul is saved.'

And he was also relieved and opened his arms, making gestures to better reassure Compare Diegu;

but his enormous shadow on the walls and ceiling of the hovel looked like a bear ready to devour the shoemaker with his table, the old shoes, everything.

The very next morning the Pons' servant Ausilia heard Nicolao's first cries while she was drawing water from the well. She climbed up on the garden wall to listen, her large feet dangling down. It was a sharp, strident cry, like a wounded animal. She jumped down and went to her mistress, saying to her happily, 'in our neighbour's house I heard the cry of someone who is going to the other world. It must be Zio Nicolao.'

Her mistress, who truly resembled a Madonna with her fine long hands and her fine long face of varnished white as though stained and cracked by candle smoke, began to tremble. Everything made her tremble, anyway; perhaps because she had drunk too much coffee; but the news that Zio Nicolao might be going to the other world also disturbed her because she realized that she felt happy about it.

'My Lord,' she said, passing her hands over her face to chase away the shadow of hate, 'let's hope it doesn't happen. How would his poor family get along? Go and see: we are all God's children.'

The servant went away and stayed such a long time that when she returned the master had already come back from his morning visit to the tavern and was saddling his horse to go to his olive grove. He also heard the cry in the house next door and tensed his ears like a horse at the whistling wind.

'Ausilia Berrina, blast you, where are you coming from?' he asked her suspiciously, because he knew that the girl, in spite of his prohibition, often went to the neighbour's house.

Ausilia looked at him steadily, her grey eyes terrible with ridicule.

'I was at our neighbour's who is going to the other world. He has a strange, unknown illness. It seems as though someone has put a spell on him.'

Zecchino let the bridle drop and began to laugh. Laughter of joy, but also of disbelief. Then he became serious because it seemed to him that the servant was mocking him a little too much.

'Wife, did you hear?' he said, going to the kitchen. 'Did you hear the news?'

'I heard it, my Zecchino.'

He had gone in seeming to want to say something; then he went out again, and only after he was in the saddle and had the servant tighten his spurs did he say in a loud voice, 'Well, we are decent people. Tell your mistress to send something over to those little urchins.'

And he went along the valley paths among the undulating white of the olive trees, under the black mountain made taller by the soft rocklike clouds. He was thinking that God is surely mysterious, at times paying immediate attention to all requests made of Him and giving such freedom to the devil. He grumbled, 'Now are you happy, Zecchino Pons?'

Then he could imagine his servant's eyes glittering in the damp olive leaves, and, turning his thoughts to the cobbler, said, 'Blast you, who told you to make him suffer so much?'

According to Ausilia's later reports, the unfortunate Nicolao had a mysterious and terrible illness, perhaps a stomach cancer, perhaps something worse; the fact is that his cry could be heard continuously and was ever more heartrending. It seemed to come over the walls and spread like a curse throughout Zecchino Pons' quiet house.

Barbara Pons trembled when she heard it, as though it pierced her heart. Sometimes when she went into the courtyard she would see the cruel servant clinging to the wall, stretching her cold red face practically to sniff the cursed air that emanated from the neighbour's house, and touching the servant's feet she would say sweetly, 'Come down, Ausilia, come down for the love of God, and take this to them.'

Gifts were sent continuously to the unfortunate neighbours: cheese, oil, vegetables, meat.

For his part Zecchino would grumble, sitting gloomily by the fire.

'Barbara, my wife, I must say that beggar neighbour of ours could take care of her husband and call a good doctor to see him. What kind of business is this to annoy your neighbours day and night?'

'Good doctors want to be paid, my Zecchino.'

'All right then, what are good Christians doing in

the world? And if doctors want to be paid, ready money is not to be found any more in the world?'

One evening the sick man's cry was so heartrending that it seemed like the moan of a tormented soul in the very walls of the Pons' house. What's more, the children were crying, too. Zecchino had come back from his sheepfold bringing two kid goats white with fat. Ausilia roasted one of them; but when the good dinner was ready, the master said that maybe he had cancer of the stomach, too. Suddenly he stood up, took the other kid down from a hook by the door, folded it, patted it, and then tossed it to the servant.

'Go on, beggar, take it to those dying of hunger. May they eat and be quiet. May they eat and let others eat.'

The servant went out into the courtyard and from the wall called the neighbour boy, tossing him the kid. Then she went back in and silently cleared the table. But the moans continued louder than usual. It's true that other sounds were vibrating in the clear air that evening. Sometimes even the dry hammering of the cobbler in his den could be heard when the smith stopped his sharp pounding of iron on the anvil. And the children were crying, laughing, and crying again. Martins sang and someone was cutting wood in the blue brightness of the February moon. But that cry persisted above every sound, like the cry of the cuckoo on spring nights.

And suddenly our Zecchino gets up and goes to the door, looking here and there just like a boy trying to orient himself before going in search of the cuckoo. He stood there for such a long time that he did not notice that his wife had gone to her bedroom and the servant was sleeping with the dish towel in her hand and a white plate with a red bird on her lap.

It was such a clear night that the kitten leaped around the dog curled up in the shed, thinking it was daytime. And then there came a sound of little footsteps from the neighbour's courtyard. Someone had opened the door and was running down the road. The cobbler's hammering stopped. Again the sound of light footsteps in the street could be heard, the neighbours' front door closing. The cry had also stopped, then was taken up at intervals, but with happy overtones. At times it resembled a rooster crowing.

Zecchino Pons had neither eaten nor drunk that evening. He felt light, as though the pure air and moonlight had given him back a little of his beautiful, distant youth. He cocked his ears and seemed to hear and see clearer than usual. Suddenly the kitten, ears stretched forward, ran in front of him and jumped high. Zecchino Pons, as though seized by a mania to imitate it, did the same; only he was less agile. At any rate he too found himself in the neighbour's courtyard and he pushed open the kitchen door.

His poor neighbours were having a feast. The kid lay on a wooden platter in their midst, and the unfortunate Nicolao, fat and rosy, sat on the mat surrounded by his children, his back straight and wide as a plank. He was just at that moment handing his wife and Compare Diegu the greatest delicacy of all, two helpings of the kid's pink brains sprinkled with salt.

What Has Been Has Been

Although she was determined not to get upset, as soon as she entered the house that was no longer her grandmother's and therefore no longer hers, but where her grandmother was still living – or more to the point, dying – big, strong Caterina grew pale. A self-willed hardness made her face purer and more firm but, like a sulky child's, slightly comical.

The deserted entrance hall was flooded by a current of cool February air and by the harmonica music of a dance tune coming from the house across the street.

At the other end of the house, through a half-opened door, she again saw the rocky garden above the valley, and it seemed to her that the light breeze blowing from the valley had come to greet her in the absence of the new owners. After dutifully looking into the empty kitchen, she decided that her

165

second cousins, to whom the house had been sold, were surely up in her sick grandmother's room. With a few strides, agile in spite of the stiffness from her long trip, she was up the steep stone stairs to the landing lit by a little high round window. As a child her bare feet and little hands knew the steep stairway well, like the granite stones of the mountain seen through the window know deer's hoofs.

After reaching the cold and well-lit landing, here it was again, in spite of her promise not to give in to her emotion, a white shadow on her face and a slight pounding of her heart – certainly because of the steep stairway.

As she put down her small bag she saw herself again scrambling up the wall with her bare feet dangling and her unruly head hanging out of the little window over the rocky valley. It looked as if the mountain had poured all its stones down into the valley to leave itself free and green like a single bush against the rosy sky; but when she straightened up she noticed that now her head was higher than the little window and that she had to stoop down to see the mountain in all its height. And yet she must grow even more. She was nineteen and still needed, more than physically growing, to study in order to get her licence from the Teachers' Training School; and so she passed the window without feeling anything; if she was already taller than her teachers, why shouldn't she be taller than her mountains? Anyway, her height was a bother: it made her spend twice as much on clothes and think that she would never be able to marry a short man, even though he might be a great man; it made her stoop to hear the secrets of her small companions. And so she had to kneel to make her head level with the head of her grandmother lying on the deep low bed.

When her sick old grandmother recognized her, she opened wide her big black eyes circled with light like a swallow's. Her feverish red face seemed to swell with blood from a feeling akin to terror; then it turned white, empty, tremulous between the grey plaits.

'Grandmother, grandmother, my grandmother! You seem like Red Ridinghood's grandmother who was afraid of the wolf!'

In fact, her grandmother continued to look at her, as grey and frightened as a sick bird sunk in her large bed that had the odour of old feathers, of a fallen nest.

'It's me, grandmother. Your Caterina. You wanted to see me; here I am. But why are you sick? You shouldn't be sick.'

She had taken the hot head in her hands and seemed to be really scolding her for being ill – she who was always so strong and healthy. Her grandmother did not answer, but looked at her and patted her hand to convince herself that her big Caterina was there, her Caterina so big that she filled the whole world.

'You've come!' she finally said in a whisper. 'What a trip, eh? Cold?'

And her hand was now patting Caterina's red cape;

167

she turned back the hem of fox fur. She saw that it was lined with wool and seemed content. Then she looked up at Caterina's bare neck, her neck as white as a marble column, at her thick hair over her ears, at her velvet beret decorated with a little rose of yellow leather, and breathed a sigh of relief. She was there, Caterina, big and alive, and she filled the fearful emptiness between life and death.

'I was just dreaming that you had arrived, Nina, but some masqueraders took you away to a dance. Now we can talk. I want to give you something . . .'

'A treasure, grandmother? Your will?'

But the little old woman had become sad. She took Caterina's hand and put it on her breast; and on that little sunken chest she felt something hard, an envelope with some paper inside.

'Take your beret off, Nina, and sit down. I have to tell you something . . .'

'Let me stay like this, grandmother, it's fine like this. Tell me . . . tell me . . .'

She removed her beret and lowered her head further. On the pillow her black hair mixed with her grandmother's grey, just as around them in the low silent bedroom, in the house where they seemed to have become owners again, the two of them mixed the sorrow of the past and the hope for the future with the shadows and light of the sunset.

'Yes,' her grandmother said softly, 'there is also the money from the house. It will be enough for you because you are clever. I've paid everything, Nina; but now I must tell you something else. Certain

things you know and remember, certain other things
you don't. Nina, you don't remember that you were
two years old when your father died, and your
mother was the same age as you are now. Yes, nineteen years old. Your father wasn't bad, except he
yelled when he drank, and it frightened poor Maria
Marta because she was small and weak. And when
he went away we both seemed smaller and weaker,
like two lost sparrows. Your father had run up a lot
of debts and they had to be paid. And so Battista
Oppos, who had been a friend of his, came to visit
us, and was a little company for us. In those days
Battista Oppos was poor, his shop was small. Then
he enlarged his shop and began to grow wealthy . . .
because Battista Oppos was a courageous man, and
everyone says he is a man of conscience, and everyone gave him credit.

'But when he began to get rich he didn't come to
us any more. He married someone who has something, who's rich also . . . Instead your mother was
poor, my Nina, and also had poor health, and then
there was you; a shopowner who must increase his
business doesn't want to marry a widow with a family.
Never mind if she is rich, but your mother was poor.
And so he married another and your mother grew
sick with sorrow. But she didn't complain. She had
been used to suffering since the time of her husband,
your father . . . Your father was a drunk, it's true, but
he was honest. What he did, he did. And when he
yelled he opened the door and window so everyone
could hear. Battista Oppos is something else; he's a

man who wants a good name; and so when your mother became very ill, he came to see us again – at night though, because his wife was jealous. And he stayed by poor Maria Marta's bedside and held her hand. One night when I came up to my bedroom to put you to bed, I heard him sigh and say to your mother, "That's the way the world is, we can never do what we want." He was quiet; then he sighed again and said, "You must give back those letters I once wrote to you. What do you want with them now? What has been has been."

'You know, Nina,' her grandmother continued after a moment of silence while the girl, her face on the pillow, seemed to sleep, 'he came because he wanted the letters he had once written to her. I had the letters. Marta had given them to me to return to him after she died. And so she said to him, "My mother has the letters; you must ask her." She called me and repeated, "Give him his letters; what has been has been." Understand, Nina: it was enough for her that he come once in a while and hold her hand. But it wasn't enough for me, Nina; it wasn't enough, my Nina; and so I walked downstairs with him and said, "I haven't read them because I don't know how to read, but as long as she's alive I won't give them back to you, and I'm a woman who keeps her word." I looked straight at him as I spoke, but he isn't a man to embarrass easily. In the beginning he spoke nicely. "Give me the letters," he said quietly. "What has been has been. I'll take care of Marta's

170

illness, I'll pay your debts, I'll let the little girl study
to become a teacher."

'His promises, Nina, made me feel uneasy; they
seemed like the drunks' songs in the street; but I
would put up with everything if only he would come
once in a while and hold poor Maria Marta's hand.
When he saw that he wouldn't get the letters he
didn't come back again. Your mother died calling
his name, but that day he was attending the baptism
of the mayor's son – you know, the mayor with his
wife dressed in silk, and he threw money into the
street to the poor people and children, as is the
custom. Everyone kissed his hand and his wife cried
at the joy of having a husband so generous and so
loved by the people. At least that's what they told
me. He came back, then, Nina. Of course he came
back to ask me for the letters again. "Here's a
cheque," he told me, "you can pay your debts and
the doctor and send Caterina to school. What has
been has been; give me the letters like you
promised."

'I looked at him and said nothing; we were down
in the entrance hall. He was serious and because he
is a serious man he never shouts. He closed the door
and told me with a sigh, "Perhaps I acted badly. I
did much wrong to poor Marta, but a man can't
always do what he wants. Give me the letters."

'Then I spoke plainly: "You can kill me, Battista
Oppos, like you killed poor Marta, but you can't have
the letters; they'll be useful to show your children,

your friends, your companions what an honest man you were."

'Then he took me by the throat and threw me on the floor; but at that moment we heard your voice behind the door to the garden and he ran away. After that I was always careful never to be alone. I was afraid, and even last summer before you came for the holidays someone tried to break down the door one night. It was surely him or someone he sent. That's why I sold the house, in order not to be alone. That's the reason I was frightened a little while ago when I heard your loud footsteps . . . But it was you, Nina. Here are the letters; take them.'

Caterina sat up, a little red in the face and dazed. It seemed like she had slept for a long time, still travelling, having bad dreams. She took the warm envelope that had the smell of flesh, illness become flesh itself, her grandmother's illness, and she put it in the pocket of her cloak. Then she got up and lit a lantern. Her grandmother was tranquil, and from the depths of her bed she looked at her granddaughter with her swallow's eyes wide and black. She seemed to be freed from a weight and was staying there, in her old nest, waiting for dawn in order to emigrate . . .

A little later Caterina was alone in the kitchen next to the burning fireplace. Her relatives, a fat male cousin and a fat female cousin, both elderly and unmarried, both religious and scrupulous, had come back from the sermon of the last day before Lent, preceded a few minutes earlier by the foolish, happy servant. But not too foolish, because she had taken advantage of their absence by going to dance in a house nearby.

'I saw a long thing pass by dressed in red; it seemed like a masquerade,' the servant said to Caterina, giving her a big kiss. 'You won't tell them I wasn't here? And then tonight you'll give me this red cape to go dancing in?"

Caterina was generous: she said nothing to her relatives, but she didn't give the servant her red cape. She was wearing it now at that late hour, sitting next to the fire. Every once in a while she bent over to look at a ladder of lines and numbers, dates, scratches, she had made on the fireplace door. At the end of her fifteenth year one date was more deeply cut than the others. What had happened on that day? She doesn't remember. She doesn't even want to remember; indeed she doesn't even want to bend over any more to look at that childish foolishness. Everything from the past belongs to childhood in the face of the present. She doesn't want to stoop over any more to be a child again and straightens her back, leaning heavily against the little chair that had been her grandmother's. She thinks that she must also conclude the business of the letters. She certainly doesn't want to keep them in her pocket all her life, like her grandmother. They are already heavy. They pull to the right like a heavy weight. They pull to the left when she changes them from one pocket to the other.

Besides, she hadn't wavered for even a second

from her decision to give them back to Battista Oppos. Her mother had promised to give them back, and her grandmother had nothing more to do with it. Her grandmother had not been able to understand that a man has no more obligation towards the woman he no longer loves. Even if the woman dies – what does that matter? In fact it's nice if she dies of love; there is no more beautiful destiny for a woman.

However . . . just because everything in life has a relative worth, she thinks that she can also read the letters before giving them back; and anyway, everything serves as example, as nourishment for our experience and strength. Besides, she had to get another envelope anyway. This one was a little worn, marked by the sweat and tears of her grandmother, and she felt it sticking to her fingers inside her pocket like the dead flesh of a burnt body. She pulled out the packet and the envelope tore, bit by bit, into shreds, like the dead flesh of a burned body. The letters fell out – and they really seemed skinned, bleeding, written as they were with red ink on blueish paper. There weren't many: seven. Only one of them was long; the others were much shorter.

Caterina began with the last; then she read the first. The secret was the usual one of love, eternal, monotonous. However, it spoke of a great obstacle. Caterina looked up, bit her lower lip and seemed to be listening to a distant sound; then she shook the sheets of paper as though to make something hidden in them fall out, and she looked for dates. She found only one, at the bottom of the longest letter, written twenty years ago.

Then she put the letters back in her left pocket, then changed them to the right, holding them tightly in her trembling hand.

She remained like this for some time, sitting erect with her back against the little chair that had been her grandmother's. Her blood was pounding vigorously inside her body as though boiling from the heat of the fire. Then little by little her blood calmed. Her neck that had been swollen and red returned to the whiteness and firmness of marble. Her hand inside her pocket ceased trembling; she took hold of the sheets of paper, squeezed them together tightly, and finally pulled them out and threw them into the fire.

Wild Game

Even though she was not expecting anyone, Rasalia looked up at every footstep. Her long head was wrapped in a greenish kerchief that had once been black, and, more out of habit than bad will, she swore at everyone who passed by. They were mostly women with amphoras on their heads and boys with cork pitchers on their shoulders going down to the valley stream below or up to the mountain spring in search of water.

It was necessary to go a long way in that drought year to find a little water. The path behind Rasalia's little hut, between the cemetery and the rising mountain slopes, ordinarily used only by shepherds or hunters, had become like a main road since April.

From her place under a cluster of tamarisk bushes, in whose shade she sought a little coolness that might break her malarial fever, Rasalia watched the black figures of little old women and young girls in gold bodices passing across the ridge against the blue background. Even rich women who had wells and cisterns at home were going in search of water.

A boy leaned over the low wall and tossed a rock into the tamarisks hoping to lure a snake out of its hole or at least a lizard; but when he saw Rasalia's greenish head, with its narrow face and slanting bright eyes that closely resembled those reptiles', he ran off swearing too.

That day – it was towards the end of May and already a fierce heat and the desolate serenity of the sky announced a dreadful summer of thirst, of famine, of fever – the path was more than ever full of people. By now everyone was going to the distant springs since the wells in town were completely dry.

Rasalia, suffering from fever, vainly spread her hands over the yellowish grass to seek a bit of coolness; she wasn't able to lie down because the blood all ran to her head, and even sitting as she was, with her legs folded and her hands around her knees, everything was spinning around her, and it seemed to her that the figures on the ridge danced in suspension between sky and earth. Many people passed by, so she had even more reason to curse. Even the priest's servant who goes to the mountain spring on a horse laden with pitchers. Even the mother of Mattia Senes, the mayor, who goes to get water in the valley spring, long and black with the straight amphora on her head that seems to graze the sky. Because everyone is dying of thirst, because they are

177

as dry as the pebbles at the bottom of the well, everyone – rich and poor, old and young – everyone, everyone who had made fun of her, who had rejected her like a leper from the community of healthy people, who had played trumpets and beat milk lids under her window on her wedding night. Damn them all.

She cursed, then leaned her forehead on her knees and cried. And in the depths of her conscience she debated with God as if He were stretched out on the wall in front of her like one of those old servants who went to the fountain, with a white beard and hood pulled back by the cord of the cork pitcher hanging from his shoulder. She was arguing because it seemed to her that God had thrown some stones at her from the low wall, hitting her on her head, her side, her feet, and at every blow said to her: 'This because you swear, this because you curse, this to remind you that you have to be good even if you suffer.'

'Be good, be good! And are the others good?' she demanded rebelliously, repressing in the depths of her soul a curse aimed at God himself. 'Why don't you tell the others? The others are bad and are fortunate in spite of it. After all, what have I done? I married a grave digger who on top of that was forty years older than I was. I knew what I was doing when I married him. But then what should I have done after all, my God, you tell me. Just tell me what the devil I should have done. I have no one – no father, no mother, no brothers, no sisters; I don't even have

178

enemies, and no one even wants me as a servant. Why did you make me poor and ugly? I don't even have a *bisaccia* for begging alms. I don't have shoes, or even shoelaces. And when I reached the age of reason, wasn't I introduced at the priest's house and the house of Mattia Senes the mayor so they could at least get me work as a servant? "First go and wash the crust off your face," the priest said to me, and Mattia Senes set his dog on me – black as a wolf. The thought of it still makes my hair stand on end. I was fourteen years old and still couldn't go to church because I had no shoes or jacket. In those days I went to pray in the church at the cemetery – among the dead, since the living didn't want me. And so Zio Antonio saw me and asked if I wanted to marry him. And I married him, what about it? Everyone laughed all right, but no one offered a hand. And boys threw rocks at us and played trumpets at night. But the trumpets of the Last Judgement will play for you boys, too, cursed as you are. Yes, God; because there were so many troubles, my husband cried with every body he buried, almost as if it were a son or grandson. And he finally said to me, "Rasalia, I'm going to America; since everyone else has gone away there's no more work. I'm going away, Rasalia, my little daughter. Over there in America there are many deaths from catastrophes, so perhaps I'll be able to work." And you know, Lord, that I wanted to go with him.

'I went as far as the port, but he both wanted and didn't want to take me with him. In the end, then, I came back by foot. I walked until I could see the raw flesh on my feet, and I came back here like a dog or cat that always comes back home. I never heard any more about my husband. He didn't know how to write. That was five years ago – he's probably dead by now and been buried himself; I went to ask a fortune-teller if he was dead or alive or with another woman, but the fortune-teller wanted a scudo and where would I get a scudo, my God? Tell me where I can get a scudo when there's famine and even the mayor, Mattia Senes, goes hunting for partridges to be sold on the Continent. And why shouldn't I swear, then? There's Mattia Senes now, with his weasel face – curses on you and whoever eats your partridges and even the dogs that gnaw their bones.'

The slim figure of a still youthful man dressed in fustian, half townsman and half hunter, was coming up the path from the little town. However, he didn't have a rifle or a dog, and when he reached the turn in the path, instead of going on towards the mountain, he jumped over the low wall and came straight towards the woman. She sat up with her heart pounding; she had nothing to lose, nothing to fear, and yet the unexpected visit gave her almost a feeling of terror. And when he sat next to her on the grass with his legs crossed, holding his big feet in his big hands like a boy, she looked at him with fright. He, however, didn't respond to that look. In his shaggy, dark face his beautifully clear, liquid eyes were sheltered under wild eyebrows and proud forehead like lakes under crags; but he had turned them to the distance, towards the little white town reddened by the sunset.

'I bring you news of your husband,' he said at once. 'Bad news.'

'Is he dead?'

'He is dead!'

She bowed her head but didn't cry. She was ashamed, or rather, she was embarrassed to cry in front of that man who had brought her the news as though it were news of an animal's death.

And yet he seemed preoccupied. Twice he turned towards her and twice looked away almost as if he were unable to look at her. Finally he gathered his courage, assured himself that no one was passing by just then, and that no one could hear him, and he looked at her through half-closed eyes, full of feline charm.

'The letter came to me, that is, to me as mayor, only today; but it took a long time. Your husband died this past winter and it seems he left a piece of land. What do you want done with it? Should it be sold?'

She became calm. Her first thought was that Mattia Senes was a man capable of cheating her; on the other hand he was the mayor, and who could one trust if not the mayor?

'How much can it amount to? Thirty scudi?'

The man smiled. It was much, much more.

'It is much, much more. I don't know exactly. And then, it has one value in America and another here.'

She was thinking, avoiding looking at the one who,

in spite of everything, gave her such pleasure. Should she have cried about the news? If many months had passed since his death it was useless to cry; but then hadn't she already done her crying, believing him dead years ago?

The man went on in a serious tone of voice, 'Rasalia, now you mustn't stay here any longer, in the grass and rocks like a viper. You are a woman, now. I checked the records and you are nineteen years old. It's time for you to use good judgement.'

He slapped her on the back to shake her out of the bewildered state she seemed to have fallen into. She started, and at last, like a tree shaken after rain, began to cry. She didn't even know why she was crying, perhaps out of joy over the money.

He let her vent her feelings entirely, until even the corners of her kerchief were soaked in tears and had tinted her chin green, then he continued, 'You must now use good judgement. You must also dress in black. A little later we'll go down to my house and my mother will give you something suitable for a widow. And I advise you not to say anything to anyone about this business. It's better for you. Does anyone come to your house?'

'Who would come? Not even dogs . . . I'm always out here because the roof threatens to fall in.'

'And yet,' he said, more and more thoughtfully, 'you must stay inside as befits a widow. All right, then, you can stay in my house. People won't talk,' he observed, but as though he were talking to himself. He shook his head scornfully. 'And if they talk, let them. There are times when everyone has his own private business. If you have problems, well then,' he ended resolutely, 'I'll suggest something right away. I'll marry you!'

She turned to look at him and felt frightened once again.

'So, damn you, it's a great deal of money?'

But he was already happy about his lucky shot. He was breathing comfortably. He seemed to have got a big partridge and was holding it in his hands still warm and bleeding. And why wait for sunset to return home with his prey? He got up and dragged her by her arm, pulling her behind him through a deserted short cut. He held her by her arm for fear she might run away.

She was not thinking of running away; she was thinking about the money and stumbling as though affected by her fever.

'How much could it be? Thirty scudi, no. Much, much more. Maybe a hundred scudi. Now I can even have three pairs of shoes, each one more beautiful than the other. Maybe a hundred and thirty scudi, maybe seven thousand scudi.'

Her mind was bewildered by so many thoughts. The man let her go in front of the church, having her walk ahead of him, however. He seemed ashamed to be seen with her. And she preceded him, after stopping a moment before the stone cross in the churchyard to make the sign of the cross. 'In the name of the Father, the Son, the Holy Ghost. You have remembered me, my Lord.'

She took up her conversation with God again. When they reached the Senes' house a dog began to bark when Mattia pushed the door open, and she remembered that time the dog was set on her. Her first thought was to poison the beast, as she began swearing again out of habit.

The Cursed House

America, it should be recognized, has offered many advantages to poor people; to those who have gone there and not become rich it has not taken away their hope of becoming so; and those who remained at home increased in importance and value. Maestro Antoni Bicchiri, for example, the only mason left to build Bonario Salis's house – without even a hod carrier – had suddenly grown as tall as the walls he was putting up.

The owner himself, Bonario Salis, was forced to bring him stones and lime, but Bonario – as he was in name and deed – had come to like it in the end. He went up and down smiling to himself and gradually learning the fatigue of a real hod carrier. Besides it amused him to bring messages to Maestro Antoni, with exaggerated gravity, from people who wanted the mason for a day's work. Everyone yearned for this precious day's work – one man because he had to get married and wanted his house white-washed, another because he had holes in his roof or a wall threatening to fall down; but Bonario laughed at them all. Paper talks, he said; and he had a paper signed by Maestro Antoni that obliged him to stay until the house was finished. No one had ever heard of Maestro Antoni going back on his word: he was the most conscientious man in the village.

Consequently, one day he thought that Bonario was joking as usual when, after unloading a large granite stone on the scaffold, he said with a wink, 'This time you have to go, Mastru Antoni. It's a matter of half a day, maybe less, to attend to some steps in my niece Anna's house. She wants to sell it . . .'

'She wants to sell her house?' the mason asked, curious in spite of himself. 'When she bought it barely three months ago?'

'It is barely three months since she bought it,' admitted Bonario seriously, 'but she wants to sell it because of the spirits.'

And he began to laugh, realizing that Maestro Antoni had become serious and grave in turn. But the mason did not like to joke, not even with the landowner. He gazed far off, towards Anna Salis's little house, isolated at the end of town. He was remembering having surveyed it himself, before it was put up for auction by the creditors of the old owners, who then all emigrated to America – men and women. The Salises, just married, had bought for nothing the small but airy house full of conveniences, and now they wanted to sell it because of spirits . . .

'Mastru Antoni,' Bonario said, serious once more, 'give me your answer. It's not a joke. I'll give you leave for half a day and that's all. My niece Anna really seems under a spell, she's so unhappy. Go and see to these stairs, since she must show it to a buyer tomorrow. You will be doing a good deed.'

And as it was a matter of doing a good deed, but also because he was a little curious, Maestro agreed.

He went that same day, during the break between midday and two o'clock, to see what work there was to do. At that time, under the blinding June sun, the quiet around the little house was even more intense. The lonely church garden, crossed by the shadow of the bell tower, and invaded by big bushes of rue and gentian, smelled like a section of scrubland. Not a soul was in sight.

Maestro Antoni recalled when he had gone to survey the house. At that time he had also pushed open the gate and crossed the courtyard without meeting anyone and he had thought about the evil rumours going around about the owner, Mimia Piras, noted for her beauty, her debts, and other things. Certainly the place was very solitary, very convenient for a woman who wanted adventure.

Maestro Antoni, however, bit his tongue as he did every time he caught himself rashly judging his neighbour. After all Mimia Piras had let the house be put up for auction for her debts and had gone to America with her brothers to work. She was as though dead and God judges the dead.

And besides, even now that the house belonged to Annedda Salis, the most devout and scrupulous woman of the town, the door was open, the place deserted. So much so that he could cross undisturbed the courtyard, the kitchen, the hallway, go up the stairs and finally reach the couple's bedroom.

The woman was sitting on the floor next to the door with her workbasket at her side, but she was not sewing. White faced, with her hands hanging down on the floor, her head leaning against the wall, she seemed ill. She did not jump at the sight of the rough, solemn mason. Only her large black eyes shone a little sadder. She was waiting for him.

'I've been waiting for you,' she said listlessly. 'My uncle has probably told you I want to sell the house. Yes, I'll resell it at the same price I paid; God keep me from taking one centesimo more. A buyer wants to come to see it tomorrow, but first I want to reassure myself about one thing. I want to take up and put back down the first steps of the stairway because there is a curse under there that has to be removed, otherwise we are all lost. I've been up here for two days. Maestro Antonio, and I won't come down again if you don't promise to help me get rid of the curse on my house.'

The man looked down at her somewhat amazed and somewhat uneasy. Curses are nothing to joke about, especially if they are well done, with a priest's intervention, for example.

'All right now, get up. Did you have a bad dream by any chance?'

'I wish it were a dream!' exclaimed the woman getting up, already a little comforted. 'The thing is that since my Paolo and I first set foot in this house we have been haunted by bad luck. Weren't we well off before? My Paolo and I loved each other like doves. But coming here was like coming to hell. We immediately got sick, first his ear and then my foot and it's still swollen. Then the horse died, the dog was killed, even the chickens died as if poisoned; then a viper came in as far as the *focolare*. But that's nothing. The worst part is that we quarrel. Paolo and I, day and night, and he goes out and gets drunk and I can't stop crying. He says it's me who torments him, but it's he who torments me. I swear to you, Antonio, that since we came here we haven't had one day of peace. We even had a fight this morning and he went away saying he would never come back. But he'll come back if we take the curse away.'

'Who could have made this curse?' the man asked, still more gravely.

'Who? You ask who? Everyone knows. Everyone knows that the Pirases, the previous owners, cursed whoever might buy their house at auction. Mimia scattered salt around so there was no water even in the well and everything in the garden dried up. And before going away she was seen with her arms crossed cursing the house. I didn't believe any of these things; but now, unfortunately, I'm convinced of it. And that's not all. I even dreamed that there's this curse. I dug under the doors, but it was useless. Now we must look under the stairs because you know that the curse works better where one puts one's foot most heavily. But I can't lift the steps up by myself. Then I thought of you who are a man of conscience and a good Christian. You'll help me, Maestro Antonio, let's make a start!'

They went. She limped, or rather walked with only half of herself. Reaching the bottom of the steps she made the sign of the cross, then turned in fright to wait for the man who was coming down cautiously, seriously, fearful of falling and yet attentive, with the practised eye of his trade, to the cracked vaults, the solidity of the walls, the steps. The narrow stone stairway between two high white walls, with light slanting down from a skylight, seemed to lead to a cellar.

After he too reached the bottom, Maestro Antoni felt the walls from one side to the other, stretching his arms. At last he said, 'Do you have a little pole?'

Annedda had a little pole, a shovel, and many other iron and wooden tools piled up under the stairs.

'There must also be an iron lever,' he said, going to look. But as she had some difficulty in finding the little lever, Maestro Antoni lit a match, he too bending over to look under the stairs. In the faint light appeared rusted tools, spiders' webs, rags and sacks and a piece of clay floor tile with large cracks. The rough face of Maestro Antoni suddenly seemed to burn with a orange flush, while his round blue eyes gazed fixedly at the cracks in the floor, almost as though he were deciphering a hieroglyphic. He finally let the match fall; it continued burning.

'Wait a minute,' he said to the woman, who was also looking, 'if you want my opinion, we can look here.'

She turned her very pale face and shuddered. She got up with difficulty since her knees were shaking. She went to get the kitchen lamp, and while she held the light, the man stooped under the stairwell and struck the floor with a large hammer. When he had thoroughly smashed it he took the shovel and began digging. The woman trembled all over, with one hand holding the lamp, the other leaning against the wall. Even the kitten, whose kingdom was the cupboard under the stairs, came to look curiously and cautiously, arched against the wall with its tail straight. It seemed to know something and followed the shadow of the shovel with its large green eyes. Suddenly it mewed, jumped, grasped a little white bone that had come out of the disturbed ground and ran away.

Annedda gave a scream.

Other little bones came up. She put the lamp on the ground, kneeled, and began to gather them piece by piece into her apron whose corners she had tucked into her belt.

Maestro Antoni was sweating almost as if he were

191

digging a well. Sweating so much that he had to pass the back of his hand over his bright, shining forehead and then dry it under his arm. But he was feeling such satisfaction that for perhaps the first time in his life he joked: 'What nice walnuts and almonds you are gathering, Annè!'

When everything was finished he put the dirt back in the hole and stamped it with his feet. But when they went back into the light of day – Annedda with the bones in her apron, he brushing his hands – they almost dreaded to look at each other and say what they were thinking.

She let herself fall in a sitting position on the steps that she no longer feared, and began to cry, passing her hand over her apron as though caressing a baby.

'See,' she sobbed, 'they've killed and buried you, poor creature, daughter of sin. It was you who were tormenting us from limbo. That's why your evil mother scattered the salt before going away . . .'

Even Maestro Antoni did not doubt that those were the remains of a murdered baby; but his conscience advised him to remain quiet for the moment. Quiet and perplexed.

The sudden return of her husband changed the situation. Her husband was scowling, ready to start the quarrelling again with that torment of a woman who was his wife. But when he saw her crying in front of the thoughtful mason he began to laugh.

'Well, then, have you found the curse? Show it to me!'

192

His wife opened her apron, and seeing the little bones he became serious again.

'All right then, what is it?'

'What is it, my Paolo? It is a mortal sin! Don't you see? These are the bones of a murdered newborn baby, buried under our stairs. It was tormenting us from limbo. But now I'll take its bones straight to a holy place, bury them, and the Lord will give us back our peace. And so be it,' she said rising and tying her kerchief under her chin, ready to go out.

Maestro Antoni took her by the arm to stop her.

'Stop, woman! You must do your duty. You must take the bones to the magistrate!' She looked at her husband. Her husband would have preferred not to have this annoyance, but he certainly didn't want to appear a less conscientious man than Maestro Antonio.

'Give me that thing,' he said, extending his red handkerchief over the step. And the woman, with miraculous obedience, slowly poured the little bones into it, laughing suddenly like a child remembering the words of Maestro Antoni: 'What nice walnuts and almonds!'

Her husband looked closely at the little bones. Then he gathered the corners in his fist and folding it, so full, and feeling it, said, 'Mastro Antonio, are you certain you dug it all up? The skull bones are missing.'

'I'm sure there are no other bones. And now let's go to the magistrate so you can be in peace.'

When he got home from handing the bones over

to the magistrate, her husband found Annedda quietly washing her apron. The fire was burning; peace had finally returned to their house. Except that she woke up in the night and began to cry, remembering that the kitten had carried away one little bone. Her husband got up patiently and looked in every corner.

'It's nowhere to be found,' he said gravely, returning to the bed. 'Be strong, Anna! We've done our duty and our conscience is clear.'

'Our conscience is clear,' she repeated to make him happy, and quietly went back to sleep.

And so peace returned to their house. And even her last remaining scruple was quieted when, some time later, the laboratory analysis ascertained that the little bones were only those of a suckling pig.

The Evil Spirit

It was October but it was still hot. From her bedroom Valentina Lecis, wife of Dr Lecis, could hear the tired chatter and faint laughter of the women gathered on the road to take the fresh air, like on a July night.

As for herself, she had already closed the window, was yawning and getting ready to go to bed.

Her husband was away and had locked the door securely, without forgetting the usual warning he gave his wife and the old servant every evening: 'Don't open the door or even the windows, if you don't know the person well who is knocking.'

In addition, Valentina was well aware of his wish that she should not stand at the window, even in the daytime, and not take part in the gossip of those silly women in the road. He held very much to the honour and dignity of the family, and so did she. She had never complained, therefore, if her sole

195

diversion was going to church or making some ceremonial visit accompanied by her husband. Or if on those warm October evenings the old servant who had been her nurse was already asleep in the same bed with the children before nine o'clock, one on each side, and all was silent in the house.

There was nothing better for her to do either than go to bed in holy peace. That evening, however, she suddenly felt restless. She yawned and gazed with rapt attention at her little foot, her interlaced fingers holding her right knee crossed over the left one. Not that she had any desire to go dancing. She was tired because she had helped the servant all day, or rather the servant had helped her decant the must that still spread its odour everywhere and she felt her head spin in a slight drunkenness. Perhaps it was precisely this dizziness and the sweet evening air and that chattering of the women, and also a distant chorus vanishing in the bright moonlit silence, that gave her a nervous uneasiness, a desire for something new, indefinable.

'What a life, Holy Mary! Always the same thing.'

She began to untie her shoe spotted with must. Her stocking had a ladder, and she was thinking that, after all, her husband was good; he didn't let her go without a thing. He let her get dresses with silk belts and stylish stockings from the Fratelli Bocconi. If she had decanted must that day it was because a good mistress of the house must pay attention to the things God gives her; and her husband was growing old working, and had his good reasons for wanting to hold the family honour high and not allow his wife or even the old servant, balding and toothless, to give the neighbours the slightest reason for backbiting.

And yet, while thinking of all this, she stopped unlacing her little shoe and crossed her legs again, keeping them slightly uncovered: nice long legs with fine ankles, her white skin showing through the ladders. An ambiguous smile, between scorn and pity, appeared on her full lips; but it soon ended in a wide yawn that made her shiver. She got up and undid her brown plait to make it smoother for sleeping, and with her head to one side her fingers smoothed and twisted with slow sensual pleasure a lock of hair that seemed like silk. She heard a light tapping on the window. Her eyes opened wide, her fingers on her hair stopped. In only an instant so many things ran through her mind.

Her husband used to tap like that when he was still a student and they made love hidden from her relatives. Her bedroom was on the first floor with two windows – one facing west towards the street, the other facing east towards a kind of open area bordered by a hill.

Her husband would tap like that because it was easy to talk at the east window. She would be anxiously waiting to see him again. He came to her like in a dream, and if the moon rose from the low line of the hill it would seem to her like a flame of gold rising from her lover's curly hair.

At that time the window was small, without bars. Her family, well-off townspeople, had no pretensions and lived with a freedom that bordered on carelessness. Later, as the family died off, and the house was left to her, her husband had had the doors and windows enlarged and iron bars installed. He loved symmetry, security, order, and he always had good reasons for doing what he did.

The knocking persisted; all the glass panes shook.

'What if it were him, testing me?' Because more than once he had put her to the test. Oh, well, she did not know why, but just the thought that it might be him, testing her, made her angry. 'I want to see who it is.'

'Who is it?' she asked without moving.

'A friend.'

The voice was unfamiliar, the voice of a stranger.

'What do you want?'

'I'm a stranger passing through and I bring you greetings from your brother.'

She twined her hair again, and disregarding the fact that the stranger had addressed her with the familiar 'tu', as shepherds do from certain little towns, she opened the window. But instead of a shepherd she saw, well outlined against the white background of the moon, the elegant figure of a young gentleman. Dressed in black, with his dark face elongated by a black, pointed beard, with the white of his eyes and teeth clear as though made of pearls, he immediately reminded her of her student husband; only he was taller, in fact very tall. She had never seen a man so tall. He nearly touched the window arch, and his open arms leaning on the bars gave the impression of a cross.

Never had she felt so mortified at not being free to receive a guest. She could do nothing more than greet him shyly and kindly, addressing him with the formal 'you'.

'I'm so sorry I can't ask you in. My husband is away... He has the key... I was already in bed because I don't feel very well.'

He looked down at her from his height, shifting a little so the moonlight could illuminate her better. It seemed that he had wanted to observe her closely and that the inspection had left him satisfied.

'We can also talk like this, like prisoners,' he said dryly. Nevertheless Valentina had the impression that he was teasing her a little, and her mortification grew.

She felt like speaking badly of her husband, but the stranger did not give her time because he began to talk about her brother working in a mine, and in the end, lowering his voice, he said something that shocked and offended her.

'I had hoped to have a long visit with you inside your house. But I can see you no longer receive visitors... because you follow God's rule!'

'I do very much,' she exclaimed angrily. 'And you shouldn't talk like that to someone you don't know!'

The man reached his arm inside the bars and took her by the hand. 'Excuse me and forgive me! Maybe

I've made a mistake. Who are you? Valentina or Rosaria?'

'I'm Valentina Lecis, wife of Dr Vittorio Lecis.'

He took off his hat immediately but did not let go of her hand, grasping it tighter in his soft warm hand, and he continued in a respectful and nearly tearful tone, 'I beg you to forgive me. I knocked thinking your sister lived here, and seeing that you were shut up in this way convinced me that you were Rosaria herself.'

Valentina began to laugh. Even though mistaken by the stranger in this way, even though captured in the stranger's hands, she began to laugh. The warmth of his hand travelled up her arm, as far as her head, and once again a drunkenness, like the odour of fermenting wine, awoke an unreasonable happiness in her. She had the desire to joke, to tease the stranger a little.

'One can see you come from a mine in the mountains and don't know the world,' she said, now also speaking with the familiar 'tu'. 'I'm really Valentina Lecis, legal wife of Dr Vittorio Lecis, but as you see I am locked in the house, while my sister Rosaria, who lives with a man who is not her husband, is free in her house. Free to welcome guests and do what she wants.'

The man did not seem surprised. He only said, in a philosophical tone, 'So goes the world.'

And he put his hat back on and tried to take her other hand. She wanted so much to give it to him, but she was thinking of her husband and deep down felt ashamed of being so brazen. Something strange, wicked, forced her to do it, however. And it was precisely the thought of making fun of her husband also, of finally having the opportunity to take revenge for the slavery that he had subjected her to, that gave her a pleasurable excitement.

She tried to free herself from the stranger's grasp, but she continued to talk to him in a joking and familiar way. 'Besides, Rosario is a hundred times more fortunate than I am. I'm always telling my husband that: I would prefer my sister's life to mine. At least to have her freedom. The man she lives with loves her and respects her more than husbands love and respect their wives. She is absolute mistress of the house, and has money and jewels. But what is most important is her freedom. Nothing can compare with that freedom. Rosaria is as free as the birds in the sky. If tonight or tomorrow she wants to go around the world she can leave without asking anyone's permission. And if you go to see her this evening, to take her the greetings of our brother, she certainly won't receive you like this, from behind bars, like Dr Lecis's wife receives you. If you want to go, go along to see her; she will open her door to you and honour you like one should a guest, she will receive you like the lady she is, in her beautiful room, sitting on a silk sofa with her fingers covered with rings like a new bride. Go on, go ahead,' she continued growing more excited, 'her friend's not in town, but even if he were she would welcome you just the same. She is free, that's everything! Her house is behind the church, a little below here, with a green door and windows. You can't make a mistake, there's no other house with a green door and windows . . .'

All at once she was silent, nearly breathless. In the excitement of talking she had come so close to the bars that the man had managed to put his arm around her waist and bring his face close to hers.

'How I like you,' he said to her; 'it's a shame you're not free to let me in!'

His breath was burning. Valentina leaned her brow against the bars and felt herself trembling all over. Never had she felt a joy and sorrow like this. The breath of the stranger went through her hair and down the back of her neck and between her shoulders like a rivulet of hot water that increased the trembling in her every fibre. Never had she felt a joy and sorrow like this.

Then footsteps were on the path behind the yard. She jumped, frightened, murmuring, 'It's my husband!'

The stranger left her immediately, going away without even saying goodbye. She closed the window and began undressing quickly. The footsteps went on by.

The footsteps went on by; they were not those of her husband, or maybe they were his, but he passed on by.

She remained motionless facing her big white bed, shoeless, with the plait undone and hanging down to her breast. She could not make herself get into bed. Gradually a sullen anger drove away her excitement.

'What a life, Santa Maria mia,' she repeated, but she didn't add: 'always the same thing'.

And a sweet and terrible hope was born in her heart: that the stranger would return the next evening. And something more terrible still was born in a deep place that certainly was not her heart: jealousy and envy of her sister.

She could see her welcoming the guest, the gentleman – handsome and well dressed like the devil is in his human transformations, according to legend; she could see her receiving him in her beautiful room with the silk sofa, offering him good wine, asking him, with the meek sweetness that had always been Rosaria's greatest charm, for news of the brother far away, of the mine, of the life of a miner. And he would look at her silently with the glass in his hand; then he would put the glass down and take her by the hands: 'How I like you!'

The man's burning breath would move the woman's light hair. He would squeeze her hands so hard that her rings would cut into her fingers.

For her, Valentina, nothing was left but to continue to tell the happy story of her sister to herself. 'Rosaria is lucky; she is luckier than I am. Freedom ... jewels ... love ... she has everything ...'

Again footsteps made her jump. She raised her head, tossed back the undone plait, with the wild motion of a young filly shaking its mane. She got up, waiting. Was it her husband? She waited for him. And just let him try to ask her why she was still up! Let him just try to ask her something disagreeable.

It was time to put an end to it, to break the chains of slavery. She was ready for rebellion. But this time also the footsteps went by and she threw herself on the bed weeping.

The next day at dawn Rosaria was found dead in her beautiful room with walnut furniture, strangled on the silk sofa. The money and jewels that her sister had envied were gone.

Valentina and her husband were still in bed when the frightened old servant brought them the news. The doctor jumped silently from bed, while Valentina rose up from her pillows in terror, screaming, 'It was him, it was him!'

And she talked confusedly about the stranger's visit. The doctor made the servant go out, then held his wife by her shoulders and forced her to lie down.

'You are ill,' he said with fierce calm. 'You had a dream and you will be careful to accuse no one and above all not to say that you opened the window to a stranger. Your sister received everyone. Now I'll put a lock on your windows, too.'

And he made her stay in bed. She wept, especially when she remembered how she had described her sister's house to the stranger, and she tried to convince herself that he was none other than the evil spirit made flesh in a handsome young gentleman. By night-time she felt more tranquil in her lonely room, because her husband had put the lock on the window.

Under God's Wing

Gian Gavino Alivesu finally resolved a problem that had bothered him for years: how to live in peace far from men, and especially far from women, without working too much to provide for his bodily needs, and without mortifying himself too much in order to save his soul. At thirty he was still as wild and simple as he was as a boy, when he was afraid of the devil, but also of God.

Once, years before, while ploughing some land to plant wheat, he had found a treasure and thrown it into the sea because of a woman. However, it was a story that seemed like a dream to him and he didn't even dare tell it because he felt it was all too absurd and ridiculous. He really hadn't thrown the treasure away; he had hidden it in the rocks on a wild coast, inside a leather purse. Sea hawks, believing the purse to be an animal, had taken it and dropped it into

205

the sea. Gian Gavino could have got it back since he saw it floating for many days just like a dead animal; but he was afraid of water, didn't know how to swim, and the place was deserted.

After that he had even gone up and down the coast many times hoping that the sea might have thrown the treasure back on land. Finally he became resigned; but in his heart he nursed a grudge against women, a terrible distrust of them. And now, sitting on the steps of the little church where he was the *eremitano*, that is, an unpaid guard, he looked at the line of the sea that rose and fell with the east wind, breathing like a human breast, and remembering his past vicissitudes he thought that finally the devil had left him in peace.

But it was enough to look towards the scrub – it, too, palpitating in the hot June morning – to realize his self-deception. For just at that moment a woman, devil take them all, was coming up the rough path, yellow amidst the green, somewhat ahead of an oxen-hauled cart covered with a rough curtain of sackcloth.

The woman was still far away and her dark shape could be distinguished only by something sparkling on her breast and belt; but Gian Gavino, heart pounding, recognized her immediately. It was her, Barbara Sau, the owner of all the land around and of the little church she had rebuilt at her own expense over the ruins of another, the ruins where Gian Gavino had found the treasure.

It was she who was coming nearer; she who is

always the same, the one Gian Gavino had known as a boy and then as a young man when he rented his plot, and then as a servant in her house after the death of her husband Battista Sau: agile, good-looking, tall, with her bright pink face framed in her black veil, her black eyes shining. She was walking quickly, her bust rocking a little like it wanted to part from her firm hips and from her slender waist clasped by a belt with black sequins. Soon she had left the cart far behind and was standing before Gian Givano to tell him why she was there.

'It's my daughter, poor little turtle dove; she keeps running a fever and the doctor has sent us here for the sea air. Now, then, my little friend, how are you? You've grown fatter, God bless you. You will kindly sleep in the shelter the servant will help you build; we'll stay in your little room for a few days.'

Gian Givano didn't even stand up or look at her; he was looking at the grass at his feet and answered in a hollow voice, 'What do you mean, a shelter! To the devil with the shelter.'

He wasn't even touched when the cart arrived with the girl – very thin and long, her feet and hands inert, and her yellow face lightly marked by the livid shadow of her eyelids and tormented mouth. Lying upon the mattress and woollen sacks that the servant had pulled down from the cart and placed in the shade of the little church, she seemed more pale and dead under the intense blue of the sky. Her mother, young and strong, looked at her with pity. Kneeling on the grass she raised her head and arranged her clothes around her daughter's motionless feet, but she didn't forget the other things of life and gave orders to the servant who moved sluggishly.

'As soon as the fire is lit you can make the shelter for yourself and the *eremitano*.' She said '*eremitano*' with respect, but also with a touch of derision; and in the same tone the servant turned to Gian Gavino, who hadn't changed his position.

'Get moving, statue! The shelter is more for you than for me. Fresh air is fine for me.'

He began pounding pegs into the ground behind the little church; but, annoyed by the invitation to help, Gian Gavino got up and went away grumbling, 'To the devil with the shelter and all of you.'

No one saw him for the rest of the day.

'Sweet Jesus, he's offended; but what can we do? The girl needs the room,' Barbara said. 'Besides the weather is warm and he won't die from sleeping outside.'

'Leave him alone,' said the servant. 'All saints are spiteful.'

'Yes, it's too hot for this time of year,' she continued, sitting next to the servant on the steps, turning every once in a while to look at her daughter dozing in the little room belonging to the *eremitano*.

In fact the wind had stopped blowing, leaving the air muggy and the sky slightly overcast. Stars appeared, distant and rosy, the odour of myrtle and laurel was in the air, and the sea in the distance seemed to pace the shore like a thief behind bars.

'But I didn't think he was so spiteful,' the woman said. 'And ungrateful besides. I kept him in my house for two years like a member of the family, and when he was ill – remember you weren't yet working for me – I took care of him with my own hands. And after his illness, because he was so weak, I kept him warm and in bed like a newborn. How stupid women are! And afterwards when he wanted to go away I gave him permission to stay here as long as he wanted, and even to plant a garden if he wanted to, without ever asking him to account for anything . . .'

'You are a good woman; we all know you are a good woman,' murmured the servant with humble admiration. But Barbara Sau started as though she had been burned. Ah, Gian Givano had also spoken that way once. And now she felt hurt, as though she had been mocked.

'Go to bed,' she said in a harsh voice, and the other one obeyed her.

Left alone, she still hoped that Gian Givano would come back. She had helped him; after all, she had felt a maternal affection for him. And at the same time she hated him.

Finally Barbara went inside and closed the door, but before going to bed she took a cruet of oil and went to fill the lamp in the little church, crossing the sacristy that was adjacent to the small room and opened into it. And at the foot of the altar, wrapped in the old yellow curtain that served as a rug, on the steps with his head on his knees, was Gian Gavino, asleep and snoring.

Indignantly she touched him with her foot to waken him. He raised his head and opened frighted eyes, but he withdrew even further towards the corner of the altar, putting his head under the cloth as though to protect himself. He continued silently to watch the woman, challenging her, but at the same time was frightened of her.

'Get out immediately! Immediately!' she said furiously. 'Aren't you ashamed? You, the guard, going to sleep at the foot of the altar?'

Meanwhile she poured oil into the lamp, but her hands were trembling and the oil spilled, twisting like an amber serpent.

Subdued by Gian Gavino's silence and fear, she calmed down somewhat and even laughed quietly, bending down to look at him and shaking her head.

'All right now, why are you behaving like this?'

'Yes, yes,' he then said, 'because I knew that you would come to bother me. You came this far! You want to take me back . . . you want to make me fall into sin again . . . Go away, you devil. I'm under God's wing . . . I . . . Don't touch me! Don't touch me!'

'Ah, beggar! Who's touching you? You didn't talk to me like that when I took care of you and you were all alone, like a stray dog. Then you licked my feet, and threatened to burn everything, to break everything, if I wouldn't become your lover. And now you put yourself under God's wing. Out! Right now! Or I'll call the servant who'll chase you away with stones . . .'

But he said no more, nor did he move, with the

210

edge of the altar cloth over his head. Then the
woman threw the cruet on the ground, breaking it,
and turned around twice, confused, as though looking for something that she couldn't find. Humiliation and rage gave her a terrible strength. She
sighed loudly, looked with bewildered eyes at the
Christ, who behind the glass in the niche seemed to
disappear in deep water.

Finally she seized Gian Gavino by the arm and
pulled him up, up from the altar steps, across the
steps of the apse, and when he tried to resist by
holding on to the wooden balustrade she tore him
free with her fingernails and continued to drag
him through the little church. Reaching the door
she opened the bolt with her shoulder and the
door with one hand while hanging on to him with
the other; pushing him with her knee she tossed him
outside like a dead body. He fell on the grass gilded
by the rising moon, got up staggering here and there
as if the ground were uneven under his feet; finally
he seemed to regain his equilibrium and shake himself all over like an animal that has just woken up.

In the meantime Barbara had closed the door,
panting from her victory, and felt like laughing at
the thought that after everything, Gian Gavino had
put himself under God's wing to escape being
tempted by her; but deep down she also felt a little
afraid. She pushed the bolt shut, removed the key
and looked through the hole of the lock. He was
there, in front of the door, and he seemed to see
her and be waiting for her – fierce, ready for revenge.

Then it was she who went to put herself under God's wing. She wiped up the oil from the rug, collected the broken pieces of the cruet, and with them in her oily hands, she knelt down and began to cry. Perspiration from the exertion of the struggle had soaked her through and made her feel cold as though a veil of ice covered her, and she was trembling with humiliation and terror because she felt that she was the weaker one, the one most in need of the warm wing of God.

The Boy in Hiding

The secret meeting was held in Grandfather Bainzone's cellar, as were all important reunions of the
Coina family when Grandfather's presence was
necessary.

Grandfather Bainzone had always been a just man
with a good conscience. Now old and nearly helpless,
he spent his days beside the door like a wooden idol
put there to guard the house. He never spoke. He
spent his time watching and inwardly judging people
on the road. He lived with his younger daughter
Telene, wife of a rich bailiff, and his grandson Bainzeddu, her son; but his other children and grandsons
and great-grandsons were always visiting him to ask
his opinion and advice about certain grave matters
of conscience, except that then they paid no attention to what he said. But the mere thought that he
knew what they wanted to do, even if wrong – above

all if wrong – soothed their conscience. So if anyone should criticize them they could reply at once: Grandfather had said nothing. And that was enough to appease everyone.

However, for some time Grandfather had not responded even to their questions: he looked at them and inwardly judged them just like he did the people in the road, and his silence encouraged them even more. Every day one of them would come; if the meeting was of slight importance it took place at the front door; if not, Grandfather, with the relative's help, had to get up and cross the narrow entrance hall to the kitchen and into the *domo'e mola*, the room for grinding wheat, then go down seven steps to unlock the cellar. In the cellar they could speak freely, without being overheard by the neighbours and the passers-by. And they could drink.

'Come on, old man. Let's go to the party,' Antoni Paskale said to him that day, tapping him lightly on the shoulder and leading him carefully down the seven steps. Antoni Paskale was the handsomest of his grandsons – a tall, strong young man well known to everyone for his arrogance.

The others followed, walking heavily. They were all wearing new suits, and some of them were slightly tipsy because it was the afternoon of a holiday, the day of Pentecost.

The old man allowed himself to be led, resting his hand on the wall; but his hard, dark face circled with a full yellowish-white beard that reached his temples and mixed with his hair and thick curly eyebrows, and his large, dark eyes expressed an inner resistance, a stubborn, gloomy suspicion. Upon reaching the cellar door he seemed to hesitate before taking out the key he always kept with him. When he noticed that Antoni Paskale was trying to rummage in his pocket he made up his mind and unlocked it, finding the keyhole with his fingers. One half of the large, solid double door was fixed on the inside with a long rusty iron hook; the other half he opened, releasing a musty underground odour and the smell of cheese and wine, and the mysterious interior came into view. To all these adults and strong young men following Grandfather the place had always been more mysterious and attractive than a similar storeroom in the house of Paulu, old Bainzone's firstborn. It was said that Bainzone kept a treasure locked in there and that that was why he never gave the key to anyone. It was also said that whoever entered discontented would leave happy, and this was true because of the strong wine and supply of aquavit kept there. All the young men touched the hook on passing, a thing they had done, fleetingly, since childhood on days the wine was delivered and the door stood slightly ajar.

Light poured from a small, high, barred window, casting a silvery brightness over the black barrels with red flat ends, sitting like a row of pairs of identical twins. In addition to the barrels there were large oil jars and pitchers, shelves piled high with discarded objects, ladders, and in one corner a tall, towerlike vat with a four-handled wine press on top of it, violet with must.

After the old man was seated on a bench before the vat, the first to speak was Paulu, his oldest son, already elderly and grey himself. The others settled here and there – all standing, however. Some leaned against the vat on either side of Grandfather, some stood by the oil jars with their faces illuminated by a dim, distant light that seemed to come more from inside than out: a veil of pallor where eyes flashed with strong passion.

Only Paulu turned his back to the light. Facing his father, he spoke quietly, briefly recounting the story of an enemy who was tormenting the family. Because of a badly divided inheritance the Coina were quarrelling with certain members of the Bellu family, relatives on their mother's side. The two families were suffering the usual horrors: livestock mutilated and slaughtered, fires started, vineyards and trees uprooted. They had not yet arrived at bloodshed, but they were at the edge of the abyss. Messengers with threats of death went back and forth every day, and old Bainzone had to watch his house carefully; the foundation was eroding and everything threatened to collapse.

'Now, if you want to hear the latest,' Paulu said, without changing his tone of voice, 'the lawyer has sent someone to say that in a few days the judgement of the court of appeal will be announced, and that it will be favourable to us. Juanne Bellu, the ringleader, says that if this happens he'll find a good way to correct the law. And then, father,' he added, bending a little towards the old man, 'last night they marked a cross of blood on my door. I've been marked: I'm to be the first fruit to fall, your first-born son.'

The old man kept his eyes steadily on the floor. With his dark hands gripping the edge of the bench he appeared to be listening, yes, but waiting for the opportune moment to get up and leave without answering. Antoni Paskale looked at him from above; then he looked around at his kin and to each one he made a slight mocking negative gesture: no, they shouldn't delude themselves. Grandfather would never give his consent.

'There is only one way to save ourselves,' continued his first-born, bending down even closer over the old man; 'have them put Juanne Bellu away until the judgement is read. That way, if he stays in the shade, he won't get so heated up.'

The others laughed; Grandfather didn't even look up.

'Now, I tell you, Father – but don't get angry. Let's do something . . .'

Suddenly he straightened up, unable to continue. He seemed discouraged by his father's attitude, and even he shook his head no. Perhaps it seemed impossible to him, too. But Antoni Paskale knit his brows threateningly – in pretence, however; and with his hand on his grandfather's shoulder he bent down to his ear, saying in a joking way, 'Let's hide Bainzeddu . . .'

217

The old man understood immediately what he was talking about, because he reddened and raised his shoulder contemptuously to drive away his grandson, who, however, pushed his hand down harder and stood up, his face dark. When necessary he was a man who didn't hesitate to be strong, even towards his stubborn grandfather . . .

'Well,' Paulu went on in a conciliatory tone, 'understand what is going on, Papa! These aren't the things of the devil. So let's hide Bainzeddu and spread the rumour that we think he's been taken and hidden by Juanne Bellu in revenge. Juanne will be put in jail. Then the judgement will be read and he, inside, like I was saying, can chew the king's bread and find out how hard it is. Do you understand?'

The old man finally raised his eyes, clear and hard as pearls, and looked at his son. Twice he pointed his finger at him, twice his violet lips trembled in his white beard, but he didn't say a word. He lowered his head again and continued to look at the shadow at his feet.

'I'll take the boy with me to my house, of course,' Paulu concluded nervously. 'I have that little place . . .'

'Ha! Ha!'

Someone cleared his throat. Someone else coughed. Everyone knew about the famous hiding place in Paulu's house – an old house that his wife had inherited from an uncle who had been a bandit for many years and had dug out that nest like a mole. There was nothing to fear for the boy who would actually like being in that 'hidey-hole'. And yet Antoni Paskale, in the spirit of contradiction, began saying, 'I'd like to take him to the sheepfold in the mountain, in the open air. There's a way to hide him better up there. Once, you'll remember, big Papa, I hid for a week in the Grottos of Punta Marina; I was eight years old! There's silver water in there, and wind that complains like it was in its own house. But the one time I was in the hole in your house, Ziu Pa', I sneezed like a cat.'

Everyone laughed. A cousin, without moving from the oil jar he was leaning against, conscientiously asked if the boy's mother knew about the plan and approved of it.

'She knows! She knows!' said another in an annoyed tone. 'She's a woman, Telene!'

'Who says she's a man?'

In the end it seemed that not all of them were in full agreement. Everyone knew, after all, that underneath his calm Zio Paulu was hiding a tremendous rage because of that cross of blood found on his door, and that he was looking for any excuse to have Juanne Bellu put in jail. They went along with his dangerous game, but their conscience bothered them a little, without their paying much attention to it – it bit at them lightly, like a playful cat.

'Now we are agreed; don't say anything, Papa. It's something that will be good for everyone. Tonight I'll send my wife to get the boy, or his mother will send him to us on some errand. You'll see that it will end well for all of us, as God is my judge,' he finished, his thumbs in his belt, his face raised in satisfaction. He apparently already saw the enemy bound and conquered. 'It's something that will be good for us all.'

'Now, Uncle, let's take the pulse of that big-bellied woman.'

The big-bellied woman was the barrel where the best wine was kept. One of the young men went to the barrel and let the bubbling red wine spill into a big jug. From the jug he then poured some wine into a glass which he held out to his uncle. Someone pushed him from behind and the wine sloshed over on to the ground. Other young men exchanged punches and two cousins who were fond of each other stood watching with their arms around each other's necks. Antoni Paskale had not taken his hand from Grandfather's shoulder. The latter, however, looked up when his son offered him the dripping glass. He looked at Paulu from head to foot and back again from a brow that shook with scorn; then he got up with a sigh that silenced everyone.

Evening fell and he remained sitting in front of his door, silent and scowling. Inside, the monotonous sound of grinding wheat could still be heard and the thin voice of Telene urging on the donkey at the millstone from time to time. Work was still going on inside even though it was nearly evening, and a holiday eve besides.

Outside, at the far end of the straight road alive with swarms of boys at this hour, one could see the mountain peaks – the one on the right black against the red of the sunset, the one on the left blue against the pale sky, with a large golden moon above it. But Bainzeddu, with his dirty little arms and his little worn velvet jerkin, didn't break away from the group of little boys as he did on other evenings to try to take away his grandfather's walking stick with both rough little hands – his pretty little teeth clamped together and his large blue eyes shining under a fringe of wild hair.

Grandfather, however, wasn't disturbed; he seemed to know that the boy was already hidden and he was waiting for the end of the adventure. He hadn't opened his mouth again the entire afternoon; not even when his daughter-in-law came later to get the boy did he say a word. The boy wasn't there.

His mother, small and weary as a little servant, came to the door to call him.

'Baì? Bainzè?'

Inside, the donkey stopped, listening. The boy didn't answer. His mother went back to the kitchen, into the courtyard, up to the bedrooms.

'Bainzè? Bainzeddu?'

No one answered.

She called him again from the street, towards the black mountain on the right, towards the blue mountain on the left; each time the donkey stopped, listening, and when the mill was silent his mother's voice echoed louder.

Some boys ran from the road, then some came from the other road, also. Women came to look from their doors and balconies. They came down and joined Grandfather with their nursing babies in their arms.

No one had seen Bainzeddu; or, rather, everyone had seen him – in the morning, in the afternoon, a few minutes earlier, riding a cane horse, with a top in his hand. But at that moment no one knew where he was. The women, of course, immediately began imagining things. The boys listened curiously with their fingers in their noses. The nursing babies took advantage of the general confusion to do as they pleased, trying to grab buttons or earrings or even their mothers' hair. Only Grandfather looked on calmly, even with a slight shade of ridicule, as he watched and judged everyone, including the babies. Bainzeddu had already been hidden by Paulu, and the sister-in-law was there, tall and slender, yellow-faced, calm and cool as a wax saint, her hands in her skirt pockets. She was there to begin the play. She was good at pretending, the sister-in-law. Not everyone knew it, however. And yet his mother was not able to keep from saying, 'My Bainzeddu must be with you.' And when her sister-in-law assured her in front of everyone that she had not seen the boy for three days, she thought, 'How well she pretends.'

She did not know how to pretend nearly so well. She was sure Bainzeddu was with his uncle; nevertheless she began to feel a strange uneasiness deep in her heart.

'Papa, Papa,' she said, clinging to the old man, 'did they send him to Paulu's on some errand?'

With haughty disdain he raised his shoulder to get rid of her like he had done with Antoni Paskale, and barely moving his lips he said only one word to her, but it was such an awful word that it made her redden and straighten her back.

In her shame she understood only that she had been terribly imprudent to ask him in front of everyone if her boy had been sent to his uncle. Secretly, however, in the depths of her soul, she felt something dimly, a regret, but not only for her imprudent action. Certainly the boy had been sent to his uncle and hidden there, and she tried to pretend as well as her sister-in-law, by calling him, going here and there in the road, going to all the doors and to the garden walls. And although she was now sure that her son was well hidden and happy in the famous hiding place, she felt an anxiety at not finding him. Her conscience leapt up in her, too, biting her treacherously like a cat that plays and then grows tired of playing and bites seriously.

People came to their doorways: questions among the curious and anxious ran from one road to another. Women calling their children, fearful that they had also disappeared. And the little mother, followed by her large sister-in-law whose amber face had faded a little, grabbed the passing boys and asked them, 'Have you seen my Bainzeddu?'

Everyone knew him and had seen him. One said frankly that perhaps he had fallen into a well, another said that perhaps he was at the bottom of the slope behind the church where there was an owl's nest.

'Let's go and look for him.'

They went. They called him from the top of the ridge; then the biggest and fastest went down. There was a moment of silence during which the nightingale was clearly heard in the valley singing a song with so many variations that it seemed like eight nightingales.

The moon lit up the velvety grass, and the parapet around the churchyard on top of the ridge seemed like a mountain, with all the dark heads of the women outlined against the silver sky. The mother and her sister-in-law forced themselves to look into a dangerous place, the drainage ditch; and they waited as if the boys really would lead Bainzeddu back up, holding him by the hand.

All of a sudden a man came running up. They heard him panting and something rattling inside his pockets. He stopped at once behind the woman.

'Well? What happened? Where is the boy?'

'He's disappeared and can't be found, Antoni Paskà!' said the mother reproachfully, at the same time watching for an reassuring wink from the man.

He didn't wink and she suddenly began to cry out for her son.

'They've taken him away from me!' she shouted. 'The enemies have hidden him. May they burn like field stubble! . . .'

'If anyone has touched the boy he'll be in trouble up to his neck,' threatened Antoni Paskale, taking off

his cap and hitting it against the parapet. 'Women, go
home. I'll handle this.'

'How well he pretends!' the mother was thinking,
and to pretend well herself she cursed louder.

Meanwhile people ran from all sides and a cloud
of boys poured over the ridge, playing and laughing
and calling Bainzeddu.

'Are you hiding under a rock?'

'Did a lizard eat you?'

But their mothers called to them, gradually overcome by anxiety, and those who had managed to
grab their children by the hand took them back
home as if danger threatened them. One woman
finally dared to speak a name.

'May Juanne Bellu be drawn and quartered . . .'

Another moment of general silence followed, and
again the nightingale's song was heard.

Antoni Paskale pushed his aunts by their shoulders
towards the house, ordering them to be quiet. And
everyone, women and children, followed down the
grassy road, black in the moonlight as a flock returning from pasture.

Far into the night the mother and two old relatives
stood in the courtyard of the house, with the front
door ajar, waiting. Grandfather was squatting on a
mat in the kitchen, in the shadow of the large oven
resembling a *nuraghe*; he didn't move, but from time
to time moaned lightly, like a dog anticipating an
enemy attack on the house.

The boy had not appeared, and little by little his

mother had been gripped by a strange madness. She still believed that her brother-in-law Paulu had hidden Bainzeddu, as had been agreed, and that everyone around her was feigning in order to make her better perform her part of desperate mother. And at the same time she felt she was deceiving herself and the doubt – or rather, moments of certainty – that her boy had really disappeared took her reason. Then she was overcome by a feeling of vertigo; but in her whirl of thoughts one remained firm as a pivot that all the others circled: that God was punishing her with that terror for her wickedness in consenting to her relatives' hellish plot.

The worst part was that the women staying with her knew nothing about this conspiracy and were convinced that Juanne Bellu had hidden her son. One woman suggested that she go at once to the authorities and denounce the guilty one, and the other thought she should, instead, beg him to return her son immediately.

She had already sought a little comfort in this last idea when Antoni Paskale arrived. He was not running now, but the sound of his footsteps was somewhat menacing. The nails of his big shoes could be heard pounding on the gravel; he pushed the front door open violently, and against the moon, bright as a silver sun, his face appeared white with pain and repressed rage. The mother looked at him and felt her heart turn cold: she felt the boy had really disappeared. From that moment she was overcome with anguish. She went out and looked up and

down the road; then she began to run. Antoni Paskale ran after her, catching her like a butterfly,
between two fingers. Leading her back to the courtyard, he closed the gate, pushed her into the kitchen
and closed the door. But they couldn't speak freely
because their relatives were outside listening.

'Grandfather,' the young man said, 'give me the
key to the cellar. I have to talk to this crazy woman.
You come too, if you like.'

For once the old man made no resistance. He
leaned his open palm on the mat and got up, dark
and heavy, following his grandson, who had taken a
copper lantern from over the oven. Going down the
seven steps he unlocked the door.

The cellar seemed as dark and cold as a mine.
They heard mice gnawing. The mother leaned
against the door, unable to enter, and began to shout
furiously, 'If you don't tell me the truth at once I'm
going to the authorities to tell them everything. And
I'll have them tear Paulu's damned house down to
the last stone. Tell me this minute that my boy is
there. Tell me this minute, Antoni Paska'. Tell me, I
say!'

Her phosphorescent eyes really seemed like a mad
woman's, so much so that for a moment the frightened young man had the idea of telling her that her
boy was in Zio Paulu's hiding place; then he vigorously shook his head and told the truth.

'It's useless to cause a scandal, woman! The boy is
nowhere to be found.'

She fell flat, face on the ground, stiff as a board;

but she hadn't fainted. She was crying and asking God's forgiveness.

'Lord, Lord! You are right to punish me. It's just, just . . . And you, Papa, kill me . . . stamp on my back with your heels . . .'

The old man watched from the shadows, huge, with his long beard, terrible and yet human, like God's avenger in the Old Testament. And Antoni Paskale was not ashamed to tremble, with a cold feeling in his bones, still in a sweat from the long sprints made to every corner of the town, and the searches in wells and outlying places. He also cursed Zio Paulu in his deep voice. The idea that the Bellus, aware of the plot against them, had acted in time really to hide the boy, to mock their adversaries more than avenge themselves, made him shake with angry humiliation.

'Get up!' he ordered the woman, touching her feet with his. 'Don't go mad. The boy is surely alive and we'll find him. We need to hide you now. Get up for God's sake!'

Telene sat up, but remained on the floor with her shoulders hunched over, sobbing her heart out, like a child.

Meanwhile Grandfather moved the lantern, putting it on top of an oil jar; and next to the jar the tall vat and wine press handles threw a shadow like a windmill. Suddenly he struck the vat three times with his walking stick, and the blows echoed like inside an empty house. Then those two, the woman and the grandson, thought they were dreaming. The

228

impish little face of Bainzeddu appeared in the space
between the rim of the vat and the arch of the wine
press. He was laughing in the shadows like the moon
in the night. From below his mother looked up at
him open-mouthed, stunned. Antoni Paskale swer-
ved here and there, looking for something to throw
at him. Finding nothing else, he flung his cap, which
caught on the wine press door.

Christ's Feast

By noon the weather had improved considerably.
Bells rang continuously and people came out on the
road to watch the cavalcade of pilgrims pass by
the town's low walls on their way to Christ's Feast at
Galtellì.

They had never seen so many pilgrims. Father
Filia, the old parish priest himself, led the picturesque procession that had to cross over road after
road and valley after valley before reaching its destination. The dark old priest – so dark and thin that
once a travelling sculptor had begged him to sit for
the deposed Christ – was riding a black horse with a
white star on its forehead. The others followed one
after another over the narrow path to the foot of
the green mountain. There were old people who
resembled ancient Iberians with their long curly hair
and very long moustaches, with hoods on their

heads and beards blown back in the cool breeze, and women with yellow veils pulled over their eyes, sitting astride saddles or riding bareback behind young men dressed in olive-coloured velvet and yellow leather. Most of the men had pale faces and long, thin, pointed moustaches that reached their chins.

Pealing bells accompanied them. People ran along the ridge to watch the cavalcade slowly disappear behind the red and gold standard that fluttered against the green background beyond the path like a butterfly over grass.

Then a latecomer claimed the attention of the curious onlookers. He arrived at a gallop on a beautiful red pony, coming from the rocky fields beyond town. In a flash, without answering the questions or shouts of those who drew back so as not to be kicked by the nearly wild animal, he also takes part in the cavalcade and seems to head it, so tall and strong is he, with his beard as red as his horse's mane.

The old man who was riding immediately behind Father Filia turns a little in his saddle and then pushes ahead.

'Compare Filia, Istevene is here, your servant's son.'

The old priest, with a black rosary looped around his crooked fingers, did not even turn around. 'He's probably just back from the sheepfold.'

'He has a red pony as beautiful as gold.'

'He must have bought it with money from the sheep,' said the old priest without turning. But his face grew dark, like the mountain beneath the shadow of a cloud flying over it like a big bird of prey.

Suddenly the weather changed. Father Filia heard the pilgrims (who had started out with prayers) whispering and the women sighing; but he continued to look straight ahead at the horizon filling with shifting clouds and it seemed to him that the sounds of the wind, the stream, and the hooves of the horses were overpowered by the clatter of Istevene's pony.

He murmured, 'Christ, God, help us sinners.'

Suddenly a shriek of terror rose from the row of women. He turned then and saw that the pony had dragged Istevene down the slope below the path. Red-faced, infuriated, the young man tightened his powerful knees about the wild animal; swearing and beating his fists upon its rearing head, he forced it back up.

'It's like you!'

The line regrouped and began moving again, but the women were agitated and the horses trembled, excited by the example of their strange companion who wanted to pass them, kicking the spark-spitting rocks.

'May you get your just due,' Istevene shouted at the pony. 'And I paid forty beautiful scudi for you!'

The old priest looked straight ahead and prayed. 'Christ, God, help us sinners . . .'

Towards sunset the weather turned bad. It was early in May but it seemed like the middle of winter.

A north wind blew and the mountains all around looked like they were floating in stone-coloured clouds, from the top of Siddo' to the three peaks of Gonare, from Monte Albo to the alps of Ollolai. If the sun managed to shine for a moment, like an ember buried in ashes, the wild flowering pear trees alongside the path seemed to tremble with joy: then everything turned black and threatening. On the distant green slopes something like white clouds could be seen running about; they were sheep scurrying in fright. To find shelter from the storm the pilgrims stopped at Orotelli. They were put up in various homes, and a baptismal godmother of Father Filia, a wealthy countrywoman who had two worthy sons, ran to invite the old priest and Istevene and others to stay at her house, and she even wanted to give shelter to the standard that dripped red water like blood.

Rain pelted the town, the wind howled; but in his godmother's house the priest was comfortable. He was given the widow's bedroom and the standard leaned like a large wet wing against the shoulders of a termite-eaten wooden statue of St Constantine.

Outside in the courtyard, in the beating rain, the red pony was pawing so that Istevene himself began to worry.

While the women bent over a black cauldron stirring macaroni, he sat motionless with the other men around the *focolare*, his coat over his knees, and told about buying the pony from an old miser who had recently died.

'Up to now the beast has been calm. Now it's

obvious that the old miser's soul is neither in heaven nor hell, but is hiding in the animal's body . . .'

And they began to tell stories about avarice.

'When I was a little boy,' said one old man, 'I took care of an old man like that. He was dying and he begged me to put on the bed a chest he had hidden under the floor. I took it out and gave it to him. "Alessio," he said to me, "go out for a moment and lock the door." I did as he asked, but looked through the keyhole. He opened the chest, took out the money and ate it. You're laughing? That story is as true as this fire.'

'Avarice is bad, like mortal sins are bad. May the Christ we are going to see free us from them.'

The old priest, stretched out like a stick on the four-poster bed, also heard the rumbling thunder and the pawing of the pony that seemed to be breaking rocks, and with his hard hand under his cheek he prayed, 'Christ, God, help us sinners.'

Later the storm let up; however, he couldn't sleep, and even after pulling the covers over his ears he could hear the pawing of the pony, the termites in the saint, and the voices of the men down in the kitchen who had begun a contest of extemporaneous songs. The roast sheep, the junket, the wine, had made them happy.

Only Father Filia was sad. A worm gnawed at him harder than the one in the yellow old saint in the shadows. Once he got up and looked out of the little window.

The moon ran among the clouds, lighting up an

arched well in the medieval street; a woman in black passed, scraping the wall with a glowing firebrand to keep away dogs that at night might be devils or wandering souls.

The naked old priest, thin as a deposed Christ, went back to bed with his mind churning, tossing and turning until he began to doze off. He saw a damp field where a herd of red ponies were kicking at each other. The flock fled in fear, the standard broke in Compare Zua's hand. Harsh men's voices and shrill women's voices suddenly echoed in the quiet night. He woke up trembling and ran to the kitchen, throwing on his cassock wrong side out.

His godmother's two sons were fighting and had already come to blows. One of them held a knife with the blade down in his bleeding fist, which Istevene was desperately holding back. The other guests were trying to pull them apart; but the two fighters seemed like one intertwined body, crazed with wine and anger, and their mother was pulling at their leather jackets, shouting wildly, 'What! What! I've never seen anything like it! My sons, you who were famous for the way you got along; you who loved each other like little children.'

Father Filia also began pulling them by their jackets, but someone kicked his bare feet and he drew back crying out in pain. With his mouth trembling he could only manage to say, 'Christ, God, help us!'

One of the brother's fingers, the one with the knife, was nearly cut off. As soon as they were separated, the other brother went staggering about,

saying that for shame and grief he would run away
to America the next morning.

Before dawn the guests left the house afflicted by
their presence. They all felt a weight on their hearts,
and the weather – once again miserable and cold –
only increased their sadness. Weather like that in
May was unheard of. The grass itself trembled from
the cold. In the grey twilight the uneven ground
covered with mint flowers looked like purplish
cadavers stretched out beside the road; the flowering
white pear trees seemed to be covered with snow,
and water was dripping off the sheep as if they had
fallen into a stream.

The once happy pilgrimage going across hilly land
and *tancas* seemed to have changed into a funeral
procession. Then suddenly a man on horseback, with
a green accordian on his saddlebow, appeared on a
path running between two walls and joined the other
riders. A joyful, slightly mocking shout greeted him.
It was the runaway brother. The cold night had
sobered him, and instead of waiting for the train that
would take him to America he had gone to his *tanca*.
There he had braided and tied his pony's tail as
though for the races, and had run to the road-
keeper's house to borrow his accordian.

'I'm going to do penance,' he said to the pilgrims,
partly to show his seriousness and partly to counter-
act their jeering welcome.

'Istevene has his equal,' Compare Zua murmured,
bending towards Father Filia.

But the old priest kept going straight ahead,

staring at the blue pyramids of Gonare against the silver sky.

The sun peeped out as pale as the moon and the water-soaked meadows sparkled like the sea; the sound of the accordian, slow, nostalgic, seemed truly like the lament of someone who was leaving his native land never to return.

But with the sunrise everyone had become happy again; the two ponies, the red one and the brown one, neighed excitedly in turn, livening up the sleepy travellers. The women were afraid of sliding off the haunches, but they were laughing under their yellow veils gilded by the sun. The old men said to Istevene and the accordian player, 'Keep your distance! The devil with these troubles!'

But Istevene was looking at a beautiful, pale young woman riding the bay of her uncle – the one who told the story about the miser.

Istevene followed closely, hauling in the reins, but his red pony kept trying to push ahead, and the bay shook an ear and hurried its pace. Suddenly it reared up on its hind legs and the girl fell backwards. She lay on the ground as if she was dead and the pony brushed her clothes with its terrible hoofs.

Once again there was shouting and jumping off horses and frightened women were stooping over. They pulled the young woman into a sitting position. They sprinkled water on her face and felt her shoulders and legs. She lolled from side to side, eyes closed, with her face blue behind the yellow veil.

Istevene stayed in his saddle, but his hands trembled on the saddlebow, and when the girl came to and was put back on her horse, he reddened with joy.

Father Filia had also turned his horse around and was looking on with rapt attention. When the procession started up again he didn't move, reining in his horse tightly. He waited for Istevene. Looking him in the eye, he said, 'You stay back. Go to the devil!'

Istevene kept to the rear.

But, strangely enough, the pale girl who in the beginning had never raised her eyes to him now turned her head slightly and looked at him over her shoulder with her wide eyes as sweet as honey. He felt almost the same excitement as the pony – the impulse to throw himself headlong, destroying every obstacle to carry the desirable woman away with him. But a mysterious brake restrained him also, and the old priest's words had wounded him like spurs: 'You, stay back. Go to the devil.'

Istevene had always been afraid of this man his mother worked for (with their holy books priests could excommunicate people), but he also respected him, and seeing him going on ahead, bent over his horse, going on and on over the white road that seemed to rise up to the sky, he felt a childish confusion.

'Godfather,' he said to himself, 'I've really made a mess of things this time.'

Before reaching Nuoro they stopped to eat and water the horses. It was nearly noon and the pale sun warmed the plain where the new growths on the grapevine looked like little pink and yellow flowers. Everything was blue and green, with a little gold and purple scattered here and there – buttercups and wild mint. And the whole world seemed made of colourful meadows and light blue mountains – so much so that Father Filia, stretched out on the grass with his elbow on the saddle, became completely oblivious to reality. He closed his eyes and slept.

They woke him up in order to leave, and seeing him look around, Compare Zua said to him, 'Istevene has gone on ahead.'

In fact, Istevene was already near Nuoro. But while his pony went calmly along, far from his companions, only turning his head a little and biting the bridle, Istevene felt his agitation grow and the words of the priest, 'Go to the devil,' buzzed deep in his ears like insects.

Houses appeared here and there on the deserted main road; only the figure of another rider appeared at the bottom of the road, a man from Fonni covered by a cloak of rough woven material whose folds hid even his saddlebag and his horse's flanks. The pony became excited again, and before the flustered Istevene could rein him in, he took off at a gallop, ran into the Fonnese, and went like lightning past the terrified people standing at their doors and windows. Istevene lost his cap; the Fonnese's horse trod on it, some woman picked it up and shook off the dust. In the meantime the terrible vision had disappeared and the man from Fonni calmly asked the woman if she knew who sold burning oil.

Heads withdrew and everything went back to its previous silence, until the sound of the accordian was heard and the dark priest appeared followed by Compare Zua with his face shaded by the standard with its sun-dried brocade resembling leather.

The woman who had picked up the cap stuck her head out of the window and asked, 'Was a man on a red pony with you?'

'Yes. Why?'

'Because his horse got the upper hand and shot by like an arrow. Who knows what might happen! Here's his cap.'

The cap fell into the lap of a woman who had bent over to catch it in her *bisaccia*. The cavalcade filed by, but the accordian played no more. Father Filia's face had become deathly pale and he beat the stirrups against the horse's flanks; the silver buckle of his little shoe gleamed from the stirrup. As soon as they were outside the town he put his hand to his eyes to peer into the distance, but along the wide road that cut through the rose-coloured rocks of the valley of Orthobene he saw only some farmers with yoked oxen and women carrying pitchers on their heads.

Not a sign of Istevene. He had disappeared with his devil horse like Lusbè, the horseback-riding demon, at the break of day.

They met up with him towards evening before reaching their goal. He was sitting on the guard rail, hunched over, bare-headed, with his hands between his knees. He looked as if he was praying, overcome by the twilight of grey clouds tinged with blood, and by the infinite solitude of the place.

White hills enclosed the valley and the road went down, twisting like a string among bushes and rocks, towards a point where the murmur of water could be heard.

The woman who had taken his cap bent over again to take it from her *bisaccia* and she tossed it to Istevene with a smile.

'Take it! You seem to be under a spell. And your horse?'

Istevene caught the cap on the wing, and clamped it down on his head. He folded it back without replying.

The pony was nowhere to be seen; but soon it reappeared, like Lusbè's, at nightfall, and Istevene began to ride behind the others. However, the pale girl who had thought about him all day and hadn't opened her mouth, noticed that he wasn't the same person as he had been that morning. He didn't seem to recognize her or his other companions; he rode in line with them like a stranger, peering into the distance with eyes exactly like Father Filia's.

And so they arrived at Galtellì. The moon lit up the castle ruins below on the ash-coloured horizon, and the conical mountain now seemed more like an enormous tomb among the ancient ruins and crumbling shacks. The smell of reeds and euphorbia inundated the air; silence and solitude were everywhere.

The pilgrims' arrival livened up the little village; the accordian filled the evening air with melancholy sounds, and the inhabitants ran to invite the strangers into their homes.

A rich old friend of the Orotellese wanted Istevene and the others to stay at his house, too. He was ninety years old, an Old Testament figure. His house was surrounded with gardens enclosed by prickly pears, palms and carob trees, and it was full of women, children and babies.

The smallest of these children, pale with black eyes, was leaning against the knee of the old patriarch and seemed a pale branch budding at the feet of the age-old trunk.

The night passed quietly and the next morning Father Filia sang the mass along with priests from the other towns there for the feast, and with the parish priest who was host – a handsome, plump young man, famous all over the district for his sermons, his witchcraft, and above all for his ability to expel evil spirits from the bodies of possessed people and animals.

The old church was crowded with the faithful: pale women with bellies swollen from malaria fevers, thin men in scarlet waistcoats, their legs as thin and straight as a deer's. The pilgrims stood out almost as a different race, and the women – though stock-still, praying with stern faces in the yellow halo of their starched veils – slyly noted the fetishism the people of the Baronia region had for their huge Christ. To tell the truth, that Christ above the altar inspired a certain awe, great and pale as it appeared in the candlelight. The curtain that hid it all year long was raised now for the sacred occasion.

Some old women moaned softly while looking at it; other women kissed the ground without daring to raise their eyes to Him. And they all prayed, beating their breasts, while outside in the small clearing the less religious men were grouped around a man selling wine and nougat, and the boys in the shade of a lean-to made of branches listened to a wandering folk singer. At the end of the clearing the green and white mountain loomed over the crumbling town, and a palm tree leaned over an old wall as though listening to the unusual hubbub in a place deserted all year.

Suddenly, while the priests inside the church began singing the Gospel after the sermon, a woman came running up the steep road, burst into the midst of the men drinking the vendor's white wine, and asked breathlessly if the doctor from Orosei was there.

'What's happened, Pattoi?'

'A stranger's horse kicked Efiseddu Portolu's grandson. The little boy seems dead. Run . . .'

They ran here and there, into the church and through the town. But the doctor from Orosei was not to be found.

In a flash the news spread through the crowd. When Father Filia, blacker than ever in his white vestments, turned to give his blessing, he saw the women, who had previously been so absorbed, turning around and whispering. Instinctively he looked over to where he had seen Istevene kneeling, with his cap on his shoulder.

Istevene was no longer there.

Then Father Filia felt a blow to his heart and sensed a new disaster had occurred. His knees buckled under him; he seemed to fall forwards, but then regained his balance and intoned the prayer with a tremulous voice like a bleating kid.

When he rose he saw the church was empty. Even the parish priest, summoned by a silent gesture, was running to read the Gospel over the body of the boy struck by Istevene's pony. The other priests had already changed and were hurrying to leave.

Compare Zua was watching over his old friend as he watched over his standard; he left the latter leaning against other blue and white standards and went to the priest who was trembling as he changed and he pulled his shirt over his head wrong side out.

'Compare Filia!'

'My dear Compare!'

Compare Zua thought that Compare Filia already knew everything, and as he helped him button his cassock, he said in a hushed voice, 'And now that that lunatic has seen that the boy is dead, he's running on his devil of a horse to get the doctor in Orosei. You'll see that some other awful thing will happen . . .'

The priest fell on to a bench of the ancient, worm-eaten choir. Everything creaked around him, over him, under his feet, in the ancient sacristy, in the whole world.

'The boy is dead? What boy?'

Compare Zua bent over to finish buttoning the cassock, as he would for a child. 'The grandson of Efiseddu Portolu, the old man who put up Istevene without knowing him. The pony kicked him in the head . . .'

Father Filia didn't say another word, but leaned his head against the choir and, while his face grew dark as the wood, his mouth twisted into a grimace. He seemed to be dying. Compare Zua poured some of the mass wine into his violet mouth, but the liquid ran in two rivulets down the deep furrows of his chin, falling on the ground like Christ's blood had fallen.

The old man did not come round . . . The church was empty; everyone had run to the place of the accident and filled the gardens, the courtyards, the patriarch's house where the women were crying around the *focolare*, where pots were still boiling for the cursed guests.

The dead child was laid out on a bed and covered with a fringed shawl, except for his little boots with shiny nails. The old man sat beside him with his eyes closed, his mouth making chewing motions. And every once in a while he put out his hand as though fending someone off, while the handsome, plump priest, standing in front of an old chest, read the Gospel – since rumour had it that the pony had the spirit of his miserly owner in it, unwelcome both in heaven and in hell.

Istevene, in the meanwhile, bent over his saddle, rode toward Orosei asking everyone where the doctor was. When Istevene found him he turned back, having decided to bypass the town and make his escape, but at the turn below the castle he found the man from Orotelli waiting to tell him that Father Filia was ill.

'He doesn't want to leave the church and he is saying strange things. Come.'

After Istevene tied up his pony and hid it behind a boulder as best he could, they went together to the church.

Father Filia, eyes closed, was still sitting in the choir, chewing like the dead boy's grandfather, but when the uneasy Istevene bent over and put his hand on the old priest's shoulder, he jumped as though touched by fire and he seemed to grow longer, terrible and grand like the Christ over the altar. He put his hands on Istevene's chest and pushed him backwards, fixing him with threatening eyes.

'Go on! Confess!' he shouted. 'In the church, before Christ!'

Compare Zua followed them, motioning to Istevene to keep quiet, and said in a low voice to both of them, 'Compare Filì! Don't shout, don't make a scene. Istevene, he's got it into his head that you stole that pony and that Christ is punishing us all because you came riding to the feast in mortal sin . . .'

246

'That's the way it is! Yes! Confess it in the church!' repeated Father Filia, continuing to push Istevene, who kept moving backwards without offering resistance. They went on like this until they reached the door, which Compare Zua had locked.

'Stop it, Compare Filia! Things of this world . . .'

'Confess!'

'Make him happy, Istevene! Confess to him,' Compare Zua advised calmly, almost enjoying the scene.

'Yes, it's true!' Istevene confessed, panting slightly as he put on his cap at the door. 'I hid it for a month, and when the owner died I brought it out. But I'll take it back to his relatives this very day . . .'

But as Father Filia, now nearly maniacal, kept shouting, insisting that Istevene confess before everyone, Compare Zua covered his mouth with his hand and dragged him back, making him sit down in the choir again.

'Be quiet,' he told the old priest, bending over to look him in the eyes. 'We're all sinners! Things of this world! Some have sinned with the maidservant, someone else takes a miser's horse, and some this and some that! And I? I have a *bisaccia* full of sins! And you? For this you have to stir up a scandal on a feast day? In a strange place? Well, be quiet or I'll have to tie you up!' In this way, half joking and half serious, he managed to calm him.

Istevene had already left, going around the back of the town to avoid being seen by his companions. He intended to get the pony and return it straightaway to the miser's relatives. Although he looked everywhere for a long time, he never found it. Someone had stolen it.